"He might hear you . . ."

"C'mon," Bennett urged, "you haven't had your fortune told yet. Now's your chance."

"I don't want my fortune told," Alex said sharply. "That stupid Wizard is totally bogus, anmd you all know it. I wouldn't waste my money on that thing."

Surprised by her reaction, they all began backing away. "Alex, chill," Kyle chided. "He might hear you."

"Who?"

"The Wizard," Kyle said. "He could have far-reaching powers, Alex. You wouldn't want to hurt his feelings, would you?"

"He's right," Kiki said. "You should watch what you say about someone who has the power to grant wishes and tell fortunes, Alex. You could be asking for trouble."

Terrifying thrillers by Diane Hoh:

Funhouse

The Accident

The Invitation

The Train

The Fever

Nightmare Hall: The Silent Scream

Nightmare Hall: The Roommate

Nightmare Hall: Deadly Attraction

Nightmare Hall: The Wish

and coming soon . . .

Nightmare Hall: The Scream Team

NIGHTMARE HALL

The Wish

DIANE HOH

SCHOLASTIC INC.
New York Toronto London Auckland Sydney

ISBN 0-590-46013-7

Copyright © 1993 by Diane Hoh.
All rights reserved. Published by Scholastic Inc.

12 11 10 9 8 7 6 5 4 3 2 1   3 4 5 6 7 8/9

Printed in the U.S.A.   01

First Scholastic printing, October 1993

NIGHTMARE HALL

The Wish

Prologue

Wishes Granted, Fortunes Told.

That was what the sign said on the mysterious booth at the back of Vinnie's pizzeria.

Alex was the first to notice the booth. Hidden in a dark alcove, it was tall and narrow. The bottom part was made of dark red metal, the top part glass, like a phone booth. At first Alex thought it was a phone booth, which was what she'd come looking for. Then she realized there was no phone inside. Curious, she walked over to get a better look.

And drew back in fear.

Inside the booth sat a figure. *The Wizard* it said on the glass.

He seemed made of stone, stiff and unmoving inside his red metal booth. His face was long and chiselled, his jaw firm, his painted mouth slightly open. His skin was pale ivory, his beard and mustache snowy-white. He wore a tall, pointed hat and a long, flowing gown to match.

But it was his eyes that Alex would always remember.

Made of glass, they were a deep, dark blue. Icy cold.

Terrifying.

It's just a mechanical fortune-teller, Alex told herself. A machine that claims it can make wishes come true.

Still, she couldn't shake the feeling that it was watching her . . .

Chapter 1

"What are you doing back here?"

The voice startled Alexandria Edgar. But it was only Julie Pierce, her roommate. Her twin sister, Jenny, also Alex's roommate, laughed with pleasure. "Look, a fortune-telling booth! What fun!"

Alex's friends gathered around the new entertainment, intrigued.

What was it about The Wizard that was making her stomach churn and the hair on her scalp tingle? Alex wondered. He reminded her of something, something unpleasant . . . she couldn't think what it was. Or . . . didn't want to.

"Look at this!" Julie cried, pointing to the sign on the front of the booth. " 'Wishes Granted, Fortunes Told!' Think this old geezer will make me beautiful if I ask?"

"You're already beautiful," her sister said.

"Too bad we're not identical twins. Then I'd be beautiful, too. Why don't you ask for something you really need?"

Both twins were attractive, although their styles were distinctly different. Julie wore her blonde hair short, in a stylish flip, while Jenny kept hers long and straight. Julie was silk blouses and skinny leggings, Jenny was jeans and sweatshirts. But their blue eyes, fair skin, and carefree, jaunty walk were the same, and people who didn't know they were twins usually guessed the truth quickly.

While Marty Jerome and Gabriel Russo carefully checked out the old booth, Julie complained, "My face is so boring. It's worth a quarter to wish for something much more interesting. Maybe something exotic, like Alex here, with her Bambi eyes and that wild white streak in her hair."

"Like a skunk," Alex pointed out drily.

Laughing, Gabe handed Julie the coin. They all watched as she inserted it, and then stood back, waiting.

"I don't believe in this garbage," Alex said more heatedly than she'd intended. "You're just wasting your money." She looked directly into the cold blue eyes of The Wizard, and her palms began to sweat.

Julie laughed. "It's only a quarter. And it

was Gabe's quarter, anyway." She grinned up at red-haired, freckled Gabe with affection.

"If I were going to wish for anything," Gabe said, "it would be wheels, so I wouldn't have to walk everywhere. My old man says no car on campus until I'm pulling A's. I've never pulled an A in my life. Miracles, the man wants! I'm so tired of walking, my legs are going to be stumps by the time I graduate."

"*If* you graduate," Marty teased.

As they watched, there was a painful creaking sound, then a whirring noise, and the arm of the man in the booth began to lift slowly.

"This is stupid," Alex declared darkly. "What a colossal waste of time! I can't believe Vinnie bought something so dumb!"

"Oh, relax, Alex," Julie scolded. "It's fun! Here comes my card. I'm dying to see what it says."

With more groaning and creaking, the arm of The Wizard reached up and out, and, a second later, a small white card slid into the opening at the front of the booth. Julie reached down and picked it up.

When she'd read it to herself, she sighed with disappointment. "Not very encouraging," she said, running a hand through her hair. "I guess I'm destined to go through life with this same old boring face."

"What's it say?" Gabe asked. "It was my quarter, so you have to share your fortune with me."

Julie read aloud, "BEWARE THE LOOKING GLASS, LEST YOU SEE YOUR TRUE REFLECTION."

"I don't get it," Marty complained. "It just sounds like one of those old sayings to me."

"It could have been written for anyone," Alex agreed. "These things are all the same. Dumb old sayings like, 'A penny saved is a penny earned,' and 'A stitch in time saves nine,' that kind of stuff. Those cards have probably been in there for years."

"My turn," Gabe announced, moving forward to insert a coin.

"Don't," Alex said quietly, adding quickly, "you're throwing your money away, Gabe."

"Well, it's my money," Gabe said cheerfully, and deposited his quarter.

"You didn't wish for anything," Julie pointed out.

"First things first. I want my fortune told. If it doesn't include a car, maybe then I'll make a wish."

More creaking and groaning, more whirring sounds followed the drop of Gabe's coin. The blue, star-studded arm lifted again. When the card dropped down, Gabe yanked it out and read it aloud. "SLOW AND STEADY WINS THE RACE," he said with some disgust. "Sure doesn't sound like I'm getting a car any time soon, does it?"

"This is ridiculous," Alex complained. "*I* wish we could forget about this stupid Wizard and go eat. I'm starved!"

"What a party pooper," Jenny said, but she was smiling as she said it. "I didn't get a chance to ask The Wizard for my Prince Charming."

"Later." Bennett Stark, on crutches, took Jenny by the arm. "I'm coming back here after we eat to ask for two new knees so I can play in Saturday's game against State."

"Get real, Bennett," Gabe said as they all aimed for an empty booth. "Those knees of yours are pure marshmallow by now. Too much football, too many tackles. You'll be lucky if you're not in a wheelchair by the time you're thirty. Coach was right to bench you."

They piled into the booth.

"This is the age of modern medical miracles," Bennett said, placing his crutches under the table. "I expect to be playing again in no time. Can't keep a good man down, that's what I always say."

"That's not what Coach says." But, sensing a lost cause, Gabe gave up and buried his curly red head in the menu.

Alex, squeezed between Marty and Kyle Leavitt, tried to concentrate on ordering. But she kept seeing the cold blue eyes of The Wizard. What was it about him that set her teeth on edge?

And then she remembered. . . .

She had been nine years old when her parents divorced. The day they went to court to finalize something that Alex definitely didn't want to happen, her grandfather, to console her, had taken her to a nearby amusement park. She had been there many times before, and had always loved it.

But this time, her attention was drawn to the plaster figure of a woman jutting out from the front of one of the larger booths. The animated figure was fat and pink-cheeked, with a broad grin on her face, revealing slightly yellowed teeth. The plaster face was frightening by itself, with its too-pink cheeks and its too-wide grin, but it was the sound that came out of the mouth that terrified Alex. As the plaster torso bowed toward passersby below, and then retreated, bowed and retreated, the grinning mouth uttered a deep, wicked ha-ha-ha, over and over and over again, until Alex's eardrums felt as if they might shatter from the evil sound.

And yet she stood there, frozen in a fright-

ened, morbid fascination, unable to turn and run. She had never seen or heard anything so ugly, and she knew, even at nine, that she would see and hear it again many, many times in her nightmares.

And she had.

Until, one day when she was fifteen, she had decided that the ugly figure, probably seen many times before, must have seemed so frightening that day only because of what the day itself represented . . . the end of her life as she knew it. The divorce.

Her parents had both married again by then, and the nightmares had faded.

But she had never forgotten the pink-cheeked woman and the ugly laughter.

And it was that image The Wizard reminded her of.

No wonder her palms got sweaty.

Well, she wasn't nine years old now, and this animated figure in his wish-granting booth wasn't going to give her nightmares.

A tall, broad-shouldered girl with dark hair approached their booth. "Mind if I join you?" she asked and, without waiting for an answer, pushed her way into the seat.

"Yes, we mind," Kyle said. "This booth is reserved for football players and football fans.

You, Kiki, are a soccer player. You definitely do not belong here."

"I'm one of your biggest fans, Kyle, you know that," Kiki said in a sugary sweet voice. "I haven't missed one of your games."

Gag, Alex thought. She's so obvious.

Kiki Duff wasn't one of her favorite people. A big girl, with short, dark hair, she was a superb athlete, and well-known on campus. Which was not the same as well-liked. As far as Alex was concerned, Kiki had never heard the expression, "Put your brain in gear before you put your mouth in motion." Kiki said whatever she pleased. Sometimes it stung. But she never seemed to be sorry when she hurt someone's feelings.

"I shouldn't even eat anything," Kiki said as she grabbed a menu out of Marty's hands. "I have to drop at least five pounds." She patted her hip. "We soccer players have to stay in shape as much as you football guys do."

Hearing a distant rumble, Gabe said, "Was that thunder I just heard?"

"Can't be," Marty said. "Too cold for thunder." But he listened for a minute, and then said, "Sure sounded like it."

The rumble sounded again, louder this time. And when it came a third time, there was no mistaking the sound. It was followed quickly by the pounding of heavy rain on the roof of Vinnie's, and, a moment later, by the sharp rat-a-tat-tat of hailstones.

Everyone listened. Hailstones could cause a lot of damage to cars in the uncovered parking lot.

"That's hail, all right," Vinnie said as he passed them with a pizza pan in hand. "Fella just came in, says it was pouring cats and dogs out there. Now it's turned to hail. All kinds of weather warnings on the radio. Wind's picking up, too. You kids should have headed back to campus sooner. Not a good night to be out. I just hope it clears up — I was planning on going fishing tomorrow." The kids all knew how much Vinnie loved to fish.

"Vinnie," Alex felt compelled to ask, "where'd you get that funky guy in the pointed hat? He looks ancient."

"Flea market. Thought you kids might get a kick out of it." Vinnie inclined his balding head toward the steel booth.

"Why are you hiding it back in the alcove?" Jenny wanted to know.

Vinnie shrugged. "No place else to put it." He smiled. "You found it, didn't you?"

"Think you'll make any money with it?" Marty asked.

"Yep. Everyone's dying to know their future." The proprietor walked away.

Not me, Alex thought firmly. I don't want to know my future. The present is going by too quickly as it is. She loved college. So many things to learn, so many new people to meet.

They ate quickly. Julie and Kyle were driving everyone back to campus, and Julie was nervous about driving in bad weather.

Still, before they left, Marty and Gabe insisted they make one last stop at The Wizard. Alex hung back, watching from a distance.

But before anyone could insert a coin, there was a sharp crack of thunder, so loud everyone in the restaurant gasped and jumped. Simultaneously, the room went white with a visible streak of lightning that came out of nowhere and sped straight across the room to the red metal booth. Those standing closest to it shrieked and flung themselves out of the way, yelping in fear as the arrow of white-hot lightning honed in on The Wizard.

To Alex, watching, the scene seemed surreal: bodies tumbling every which way, the booth radiating white light, startled shouts and cries, a sizzling sound, and then an unmistakable burning smell.

And then, as she cringed in fear against the wall, The Wizard went dark and every light in the restaurant went out.

There were shouts of dismay and cries of fear. A sudden, eerie silence descended upon the room.

And although his image had completely disappeared into the veil of darkness, Alex could still feel the icy blue eyes of The Wizard, watching, watching . . .

Chapter 2

In the black silence that had overtaken the restaurant, a voice said in a near-whisper, "What was that?"

Marty, picking himself up from the floor, answered, "I think it was lightning."

"Anyone hurt?" Vinnie called out.

No one seemed to be. But they were all severely shaken.

"Everybody stay cool," Vinnie called. "Don't try moving around until the lights come back on."

An air of nervous excitement filled the room. No one seemed anxious to leave, in spite of the darkness surrounding them. The sharp rat-a-tat-tat sound had ended, but heavy rain continued to pound down upon the roof.

"Bennett," Marty called, "the four of us were closest to where it struck. You and Kyle okay? What about Gabe?"

"Not a scratch. Never better."

Alex stood against the wall, watching, listening. They all seemed to be enjoying the excitement. All she wanted to do was get out of there. Fast. It wasn't the darkness that bothered her as much as what was in it. She couldn't see The Wizard, but she could feel those eyes. Her earlier resolution about not letting him bother her disappeared.

"Why don't we just go?" she asked. "The electricity might not come back on tonight, and stumbling around this place in the dark isn't my idea of a good time. If the lightning only struck here, there'll be lights on campus."

She had just finished speaking when the restaurant was flooded with light. A chorus of cheers rang out.

Alex's eyes were drawn, involuntarily, to the fortune-telling booth. Except for a faint scorch mark on his hat, The Wizard seemed undamaged. No one else close to the booth had been injured, either. The lightning hadn't been as dangerous as it had looked.

After a moment or two, everyone resumed what they'd been doing when the storm hit.

"Let's go," Alex repeated. "Before the lights go out again."

"Wait!" Kiki cried, "I want to try The Wizard. I'm going to wish I were five pounds thinner."

But no one had any quarters left, and Alex was already on her way out the door.

Disgruntled, Kiki followed along.

The minute Alex stepped outside, she felt an enormous sense of relief.

The rain had tapered off to a light drizzle, and the night sky overhead was beginning to clear.

Marty, Alex, and Jenny climbed into the backseat of Julie's car, while Gabe, after failing to persuade Julie to let him drive, climbed in beside her. Bennett and Kiki rode with Kyle in his pickup truck.

Alex was acutely conscious of Marty sitting beside her in the backseat. He was nice, and had a great sense of humor, but she hardly knew him. There hadn't been time to get to know anyone really well, except her roommates, the twins. They'd been a big help. They were a lot more outgoing than she was, and she was learning from them.

Maybe, if she asked them, they could tell her if Marty was interested in her. Maybe they were better at figuring out things like that than she was. She didn't have a clue.

Evidence of the brutal storm littered the parking lot. The globes of many of the pole lights had been shattered by hailstones, leaving the area in a dismal semidarkness. Shopping receipts and paper bags clung to windshields, blown there by an angry wind.

"Looks like a war zone," Marty commented as they drove out of the parking lot. Tree limbs and broken branches and road signs dotted the highway like body parts.

Halfway to campus, they passed Nightingale Hall, an off-campus dorm sitting high on a hillside. An old brick house nearly hidden in shadows cast by huge old oak trees, it had been nicknamed *"Nightmare* Hall" following the tragic death of a female student who lived there. Rumors circulated of strange things happening there. People said it was haunted.

"Now there's a place I wouldn't want to spend a stormy night," Marty said as they passed.

"Well, at least the lights are on," Alex said. "That should mean we'll have electricity on campus, too."

They could see as they passed that at least two of the windows had been blown out of Nightingale Hall, leaving gaping wounds in the structure.

"Wow," Julie breathed as she steered around debris, "Mother Nature really went on a rampage tonight. I'm glad we were inside, and safe."

Alex's immediate, unspoken response was, How safe were we, really? And then she wondered why she'd thought it.

Probably because of the electricity going out. She hated darkness. She didn't find it romantic or comforting, the way some people did. She had brought a night light with her to college, a pretty, softly glowing crystal hummingbird that plugged into an electrical outlet. The twins had never mentioned it, for which Alex was grateful.

No, she didn't like being in the dark, not at all. Darkness didn't seem . . . kind.

Now, Alex watched the road carefully, peering out over the front seat through the mist-moistened windshield, watching for objects in the road. Julie was talking to Gabe about the new fortune-telling booth, and she occasionally glanced in his direction. Alex didn't think that was such a hot idea. With all that stuff on the road, Julie should be watching every single second.

"Well," Julie said, steering carefully around a broken tree limb lying in the highway, "The Wizard didn't promise to make me beautiful this time, but there's always a next time. If at first you don't succeed. . . ."

"I think he's creepy," Alex said, not taking her eyes off the highway for a second. "Those eyes give me the chills."

"Everything gives you the chills," Jenny said. "You still sleep with a nightlight."

Alex was caught completely off guard. She couldn't believe Jenny had revealed to everyone in the car, including Marty, that she was afraid of the dark. Well . . . not *afraid* of . . . not really. *Uncomfortable* with, was a better way of putting it. She wasn't comfortable in total darkness, that was all.

So what? Julie was terrified of spiders, and Kyle was afraid of heights. It was all the same thing. Still, it wasn't the kind of thing a college freshman wanted to advertise.

Shrugging, Alex returned her attention to the highway stretched out like a long gray ribbon in front of Julie's headlights. They were closer to campus now, and there seemed to be less debris.

She couldn't wait to get back to the safety and comfort of their dorm room. Thanks to Jenny's creativity, Julie's efficiency, and Alex's generous stepfather, it was one of the prettiest and nicest rooms in Lester. Alex's favorite thing in the room was the huge rainbow they'd painted on one of the walls one Saturday, each girl painting a different color: salmon-pink, turquoise, and yellow.

That rainbow was beckoning to her now, calling her back to safety and comfort.

"Almost there," Julie said cheerfully, turning her head slightly toward the passengers in the backseat. Her attention was away from the road for only a second, but that was a second too long.

Alex saw the tree before anyone else did.

Too late, she screamed a warning.

Julie gasped and slammed on the brakes. In vain.

The car plowed into the upper half of a mammoth old tree lying across the road, a thick black barrier. Its fat, leafless branches reached up and out like grasping hands. Just before impact, one of the branches punched its way through the windshield, showering the car's interior with glass.

Julie cried out, her hands flying to her face.

Then they hit, hard.

The impact flung the upper part of Julie's body forward. Her head slammed into the steering wheel, bounced back against the seat, and ricocheted forward a second time. Then she lay still, her arms hanging limply at her sides, her bloodied face resting against the steering wheel.

At the same moment, the front of the car crumpled inward like an accordion, driving twisted metal backward, straight into Gabe's legs. He screamed just once before passing out, his head flopping loosely against the back of the seat.

The passengers in the backseat were flung forward, too, in spite of their seat belts. Their faces slammed into the back of the front seat and then bounced backward, as Julie's had.

The car, pinioned by the tree branch in the windshield, skidded sideways just once, and then came to a rest, sideways in the road.

Behind it, Kyle's truck shrieked to a halt.

Chapter 3

No one in the car moved. No one made a sound. Gabe and Julie were unconscious, and the back-seat passengers had been stunned into a frozen silence.

Tiny spots of black and orange whirled around Alex's head. She shook it, trying to erase the spots. Her ears rang, and she couldn't remember where she was. What was she doing in this car? Shouldn't she be home in bed?

Oh. She didn't live at home anymore. She lived on campus. With twins.

The girl sitting beside her . . . Alex decided this girl was probably one of the twins . . . sat up with a groan and called out a name.

Julie. The name she called was Julie. Her sister, Alex thought. Her twin sister. The driver . . . the girl whose face wasn't there anymore. Her head was lying on the steering wheel, but her eyes were closed and everything else was all smeared together in a sort of bright red mess.

When the twin in the backseat got no response, her voice rose to a scream.

The boy beside Alex, cursing softly, struggled with his seat belt.

A boy's face appeared at the front window on the passenger's side. Alex had no idea who he was. Someone called out, "Kyle! Get us out of here!" So she thought the boy's name must be Kyle. Did she know someone named Kyle? She couldn't remember.

The black and orange spots continued to spin, like a constellation, around Alex's head.

A different face appeared at the driver's window. Now there were two people on the outside of the car, both struggling to open a door. A girl joined them. She, too, wrestled with the door handles.

Feeling detached, as if none of this had anything to do with her, Alex thought, That girl will get us out. She looks strong enough to open just about anything.

There were three people struggling to get the car doors open. None was having any luck. The doors remained solidly jammed.

"I want *out* of this car right now!" Alex said aloud.

The twin on her right was sobbing.

It was a two-door car, and the half-windows in the back didn't open at all. When the boy beside Alex finally got free of his seat belt, he got up and pushed past her to attempt to open the front window. But the windows were electric, sealed shut.

His arm brushed against the head of the injured boy in the front seat, and the boy moaned.

Groaning in defeat, the boy who had tried to open the window flopped back into his seat and put his head in his hands. "God," he said, "is that gasoline I smell?"

Alex pretended she didn't smell a thing. The girl beside her was already hysterical. What would she do if she thought the car might catch on fire at any second?

But Alex did smell gasoline. Were they all going to be burned alive?

Someone was shouting . . . one of the boys outside the car had pressed his face against the window and was hollering something. Alex thought his face looked really funny, all smashed against the glass like that, like a pumpkin discarded after Halloween.

"Kiki called the fire department!" she heard.

Who was Kiki?

"The firemen will get you out," the mouth in the mashed face continued. "Hang in there.

They're bringing an ambulance, too." Then the mouth added, "Is Jenny okay?"

Jenny? The twin, sobbing hysterically. Jenny was definitely not okay.

The Jenny who was not okay leaned over the front seat and began to shake the driver, trying to awaken her.

Alex snapped out of her fog to grab Jenny's arm. "Stop that right now!" she cried. "Don't touch her! She could have a neck injury, or a spinal thing. You're not ever supposed to move anyone when they've been in an accident."

The words surprised . . . astonished her. An accident? Is that what was happening? They had had an accident?

How had it happened?

Why had it happened?

Was anyone dead?

"Is anyone dead?" Alex said aloud, and then laughed, because of course if someone were dead, they wouldn't be answering her, would they?

The boy who had tried to open the window was looking at her funny.

She probably shouldn't be laughing when they'd just had an accident.

The black and orange spots disappeared. They were immediately replaced by a blinding headache. Alex closed her eyes. The gasoline smell made her stomach churn.

The loud wail of approaching sirens seemed as if it would split her skull in two. But she knew it was a good sound, a sound they'd been waiting for.

It took firemen in yellow slickers, shiny as patent-leather, ten long, agonizing minutes to remove the seriously wounded passengers from the front seat, clearing a path for the three in the back seat to fumble their way to freedom and fresh air.

The cool, clean air cleared Alex's head a little. They'd had an accident. A bad one. Julie, her roommate, was hurt. Gabe, Julie's boyfriend, was hurt, too. And the boy who had tried to open the front window was Marty, and the twin in the back seat was Jenny, another roommate. Alex didn't think she had more than two roommates, but she wasn't sure.

There were many cars parked along the roadway, and people, most of them students, stood on the grass watching the firemen hose away the gasoline.

They're glad they weren't in this car, Alex thought. They're sorry for us, but they're glad it wasn't them.

She didn't blame them.

Although she insisted repeatedly that she

was fine, just fine, Alex was loaded into an ambulance with Marty and Jenny, Julie and Gabe were placed in another ambulance. Sirens screamed again as both vehicles spun around and headed back toward the community hospital in Twin Falls.

The doctor in the emergency room found nothing more than a bruise on Alex's forehead and a deep scratch on her neck from flying glass.

"I didn't know what was happening," she admitted with some embarrassment. "I mean, I was really out of it back there. I thought maybe it meant that something had happened to my head."

"That was your mind protecting you from the knowledge that something terrible had happened," he explained. "Perfectly normal. Too bad we can't escape like that all the time, right?"

Alex didn't agree. It had been awful not knowing what was going on.

She came out of the emergency room just as Marty did.

"You okay?" he asked, taking her elbow.

Alex winced. Another bruise. "I'm fine. Are you?"

He nodded. But she noticed he was limping slightly.

Together, they walked to the waiting room, anxious for word of Julie and Gabe. The stuffy little room was crowded.

"Where's Jenny?" Alex asked Kyle, who met them at the door, two cups of hot coffee in hand. He handed a cup to each of them.

"Still in the emergency room with Julie. No one's told us a thing about Julie. But Gabe's already on his way to surgery. His legs are a mess."

Feeling suddenly faint, Alex sank into an orange plastic chair. "But Julie's okay, right?"

"Don't know yet." Kyle leaned his bulk against the wall. "It's Jenny I'm really worried about. She wouldn't even let a doctor look at her. She didn't want to leave Julie. I guess they let her stay in there, because she never came back out."

Then Kyle told her that Bennett had broken one of his crutches trying to break a window to get them out of the car.

For a moment, Alex couldn't remember who Bennett was, and worried again that her brain had been dislodged when her head slammed into the back of the front seat. But then her eyes focused on a big, blond guy in jeans and a Salem U sweatshirt, standing beside Marty. He was leaning casually on one crutch as if he'd brought it because he liked the way it looked, not because he needed it.

Catching her eye, Bennett hip-hopped on his crutch over to stand by her chair. "Gabe won't be playing football for a while," he said.

Alex looked up at him in alarm. "What are you talking about? Have you heard something?"

"No. But I saw his legs when they pulled him out of the car."

The girl Alex now recognized as Kiki was not so delicate. "His legs looked like they'd been attacked by a power mower," she said bluntly. Then her voice hardened. "Why wasn't Julie paying more attention?"

Shocked, Alex cried, "You can't possibly blame Julie! It wasn't her fault." Julie certainly hadn't planned to smash up her car . . . and her face.

Just then Jenny appeared in the doorway. Her face was mushroom-colored and she swayed dangerously.

Kyle rushed over to lead her to a chair. The others gathered around, eager to hear about Julie's condition.

Jenny had difficulty getting the words out, as if saying them aloud would make them real and she couldn't bear that. She twisted the edge of her gray university sweatshirt as she struggled to speak.

"Her face . . . her face . . . she hit the steering wheel so hard . . . and when the windshield shattered . . . she has so many cuts . . ." Her blue eyes were bleak, the edges rimmed scarlet from her tears. "The doctor said . . . he said most of the bones in her face were broken . . . her jaw is fractured, and one cheekbone . . ." She couldn't continue. She covered her face with her hands.

No one spoke. The dismal news had rendered Julie's friends speechless with horror.

Jenny lifted her head. Her eyes, full of pain, moved to Alex's face. "Oh, Alex," she said so quietly that Alex had to bend her head to hear, "Julie's beautiful face, the one she said was so boring . . . it's ruined. It will never look the same again."

Then she leaned back against the seat and closed her eyes.

No one knew what to say.

They all waited together. But there was no further word about Julie or Gabe.

Jenny refused to leave the hospital. The doctors and nurses assured her that Julie would probably sleep through the night. Alex and Marty reminded Jenny that she'd had a bad time herself and needed some rest. Kyle told her gently that she wouldn't be any help to Julie if she herself was exhausted.

Their efforts were futile.

"I'm going to be there when my sister wakes up," Jenny said firmly, her face bleached white, an ugly purplish bruise forming on her forehead. "Whenever that is, I'm going to be there."

Giving in, one of the nurses arranged for a cot to be installed in Julie's room, and led Jenny away.

Alex's expression was forlorn as she watched them leave. She wanted to stay, too. Her roommates were in pain. How could she just walk away? But she wasn't a member of the family. She would have to go back to the dorm . . . alone.

Kyle drove them home. No one talked on the way.

Alex sat staring out the window, unseeing. There had never been a darker, more vicious night, as far as she was concerned. When they drove by the accident scene, she began to shake violently. Julie's car was gone, but skid marks were clearly visible on the highway. Bits of broken glass sparkled like jewels in Kyle's headlights. The cruel tree branch that had impaled the windshield lay beside the road, its grasping black claws reaching up and out.

Waiting for another victim. Alex wrapped her arms around her chest and pulled her eyes away from the road, staring down at her lap instead.

Without Jenny and Julie, room 614 in Lester dorm seemed cold and forbidding, like the night outside.

Seeing the bleak expression on Alex's face as she stood in the doorway, Marty offered to stay with her. "If you think you won't be able to sleep, we could talk. And we could call the hospital every once in a while to see if there's any word about Gabe or Julie."

Alex shook her head. "Thanks. But I'll be fine. You could help tomorrow, though, by giving me a ride into town. I want to get flowers, and maybe some magazines for Gabe and Julie. There's a nice flower and gift shop right next door to Vinnie's. If it wasn't struck by lightning," she added darkly.

"Sure. What time?"

Since neither had a ten o'clock class, they settled on nine-thirty.

Before he left, Marty put a hand on her shoulder and smiled down at her. "You sure you're not going to sit here obsessing about what happened? You're going to get some sleep, right?"

Grateful for his concern, Alex returned the smile. "Right." She sighed. "I think I could sleep for a year right about now."

His smile disappeared, and he nodded grimly. "Right. See you in the a.m."

When he had gone, the emptiness of the room, in spite of its clutter, seemed to shout the twins' absence. Alex stood by the open door, watching Marty walk, limping, down the hallway. In her mind, she saw the accident again, watched as his head snapped forward and back. She winced.

Alone in her room, she slipped off her jacket, and without changing out of her jeans, blouse, and suede vest, collapsed on her bed. When she closed her eyes in the dark, quiet room in the dark, quiet building, her head began to throb. She saw again the anguish in Jenny's face as she'd told all of them that Julie's face would never be the same. And quiet tears began to streak her own face.

Plastic surgeons could work miracles, couldn't they? Was Julie going to need a miracle?

Just before she finally fell into an exhausted sleep, Alex remembered Julie's comments at Vinnie's. What was it she had said? Something about being sick of her "boring old face"? It wouldn't be the same old boring face now, would it?

But the face that appeared then in Alex's semiconscious mind wasn't Julie's. It was the dark, chiselled face of The Wizard.

And he seemed to be smiling.

Chapter 4

Alex awoke early the next morning to a bruised and aching body. Her left eye was encircled in purple, her lower lip swollen and painful. Showering and dressing was agony. Her jeans hurt her legs, and the soft blue turtleneck sweater she slipped on felt like rough wood against her aching neck.

When she called the hospital, she was told that information about Ms. Pierce and Mr. Russo could only be given to relatives.

I should have said I was Julie's mother, Alex thought sourly as she hung up. Why wasn't a roommate and best friend as important as a relative? Not fair.

Marty arrived on time. He, too, moved stiffly, his customary confident swagger defeated by aching muscles. Purple bruises streaked his cheekbones and discolored his strong, square jaw.

He greeted her with a gentle hug. "Sleep at all?"

She nodded. "But I can't find out anything about Julie and Gabe. Have you heard anything?"

"No. We're not going to learn anything unless we go to the hospital. We can do that after we get the flowers and stuff."

That lifted Alex's spirits a little. It was good to have a plan. "Maybe we can drag Jenny away from there." Then she added quickly, "If Julie's okay, I mean."

She averted her eyes when they passed the accident scene again. But not before she saw that although the glass had been removed or had blown away, the black, bare tree limb still lay in the ditch by the side of the road.

"Hold on," Marty said, sensing her tension, "we'll be past in a sec."

And they were. But Alex knew she would have to pass that site many times. Would she ever reach the point where seeing it wouldn't bother her? That seemed impossible now. Maybe, if Julie and Gabe weren't hurt as seriously as everyone thought they were, maybe after a while she could drive right by that spot without cringing.

If Julie and Gabe were okay.

They bought a white wicker basket filled

with rust, yellow, and orange flowers for Julie, and a bouquet of brightly colored balloons for Gabe. They were leaving the gift shop just as Kiki Duff came out of Vinnie's, a large white pizza box in hand. Kyle and Bennett were right behind her.

"This isn't for me," Kiki cried. "I really am on a diet, honest! This is for Gabe. He called Bennett and asked for it, so I guess he's feeling better."

That was good news.

And Bennett was walking without crutches.

"I guess you're better, too," Alex commented as they all headed for their vehicles in the parking lot. "No crutches? Did you toss them?"

"Had to. With Gabe out, Salem needs all the help it can get. I can't sit around nursing my lumps when the team's in trouble. My knees are fine."

Medical miracle? Alex wondered, but she said nothing. Bennett wasn't a stupid person. He wouldn't play — and Coach Jeffers wouldn't let him — unless he really was okay.

"Here, look at this!" Kiki said, handing the pizza box to Bennett and pushing something toward Alex.

It was a small, white card.

Alex recognized it instantly. It was from the fortune-telling machine.

"You had your fortune told?"

Kiki grinned. "Yep. Go ahead, read it!"

Alex read, SELF-DISCIPLINE IS THE GREATEST OF ALL VIRTUES.

She handed the card back to Kiki. "You wasted a quarter. My grandmother used to tell me the same thing when I wouldn't clean my room, and she didn't charge me for it."

"Well, don't you get it?" Kiki said. "It's like he knew I wanted to go on a diet, and didn't have the self-discipline to do it."

Alex made a sound of disgust. "Kiki, for pete's sake! Someone who weighs ninety pounds and doesn't have an ounce of fat on her could have got that card."

"Yeah, but she didn't. *I* got it. And I don't weigh ninety pounds. But I will now. I've already started my diet, and I'm going to stay on it this time."

Alex knew she wouldn't. Kiki was always going on a diet of one kind or another, and never stuck to it for more than a few days. "If you weighed ninety pounds," Alex said as she climbed into Marty's car, "you'd look like a twig. You're too tall to weigh that." That was probably Kiki's trouble. She dieted briefly, in hopes of looking petite, like the twins, and then got so discouraged when it didn't happen, that she fell off her diet.

The same thing would probably happen this time, in spite of the little white card.

At the hospital, they were told that Julie was not allowed visitors. But the nurse agreed to phone her room so Alex could talk to Jenny.

She sounded very tired. "Julie's still not awake. She has a concussion. The doctor keeps telling me that it's okay, her sleeping like this, but it scares me. Can you come up?"

"They won't let us. Can you come up to Gabe's room? He's allowed visitors, so we're all going up there. It's room 312."

When Jenny stepped out of the elevator on the third floor where Alex was waiting, Alex's heart sank. She looked terrible. Her face was bruised and swollen, and she obviously hadn't slept. When Alex hugged her, Jenny said, "I've tried to contact my parents. They're in Ireland on a vacation they'd planned for years. How can I tell them what's happened? I just left a message. Can we go in and see Gabe now? Maybe that will cheer me up."

Gabe was grinning at something someone had said when Alex and Jenny walked in. But his freckles stood out like neon dots on a face as white as his pillowcase. Both legs, lying above the sheet, were swathed in white. "Join the feast," he told the girls. "No one came empty-handed."

The pizza from Vinnie's was being passed around, along with boxes of huge, fresh cookies and chocolate candy. Gabe insisted that everyone help themselves.

Kiki, a fat chunk of chocolate halfway to her mouth, looked at Alex with a guilty grin. "Tomorrow," she announced, "tomorrow I start my diet, absolutely."

Alex had to smile. So much for the message about self-discipline on The Wizard's card.

Gabe seemed much better than they'd expected, and the atmosphere in his room was like a party. Until he asked Jenny, "So where's your better half? In bed with a killer of a headache, I'd bet. I saw her head slam into that steering wheel before my own lights went out. She hit it hard. Is she sleeping it off? She'll be in to see me this afternoon, though, right?"

Alex froze. Oh, no. No one had told Gabe about Julie? And then she realized that of course the medical staff wouldn't have told him, not wanting to upset him. And Jenny had been downstairs in Julie's room all night and morning. Even if she'd had the chance, telling Gabe would have been far too painful for Jenny.

A miserable silence filled the room. Gabe

picked up on it right away. "She's hurt?" he asked. "Bad?"

"Gabe," Marty began, moving closer to the bed, but Kiki interrupted him.

"It's her face," she said bluntly. "Smashed." She bit into a giant chocolate chip cookie. "Probably never be the same."

"Kiki!" Alex cried as Jenny paled and clutched the wall for support.

Kiki shrugged. "No point in lying to him. He'll see for himself soon enough."

Gabe frowned. "Well, she's not in a coma, or crippled or anything, is she? I mean, except for her face, she's okay, right?"

"No, no coma," Jenny assured him. Some of the color returned to her face. "She's not awake yet, but they keep telling me she will be, any minute now."

"Just don't give her a mirror," Kiki mutterd, reaching for the candy box.

"Kiki," Kyle said in a calm, polite voice, "have some candy. It'll keep your mouth occupied."

While Gabe and Jenny talked quietly about Julie, Marty steered the conversation to happier subjects. Soon they were talking about that week's football game. Alex would go to the game Saturday — she wasn't a big football fan, but she always went to see her friends

41

play. Gabe and Bennett, Kyle and Marty were all freshmen, but they were good. So they'd played some. Not enough to satisfy them, but more than most freshmen. They were a part of the team, and it seemed important to be there for them. They all hated having so little play time. They had all complained about it.

Alex thought she understood. It was hard enough being a freshman, after being a bigshot high school senior. It must be even worse if you'd spent three or four years being a hotshot football star . . . getting your name in the paper and on the local news, going to banquets held in your honor, dating the prettiest and most popular girls in school because you were a bigdeal athlete. And then getting to college where there were tons of guys just as good as you were, some of them bigger, some older. The upperclassmen got most of the playing time on the football field.

"At least we all made the team," Marty had told her after a party a week or so ago. "There are guys here who were really big deals in high school, and they didn't last a week here. I have nightmares about that happening."

Gabe was asking Jenny which room Julie was in. "If they ever let me out of this bed," he said, shifting his weight with a painful grimace, "I'll hike on down to see her. She's probably scared." He smiled halfheartedly. "This is a very scary place."

Jenny was just about to tell him Julie's room number, when a nurse appeared in the doorway. "Miss Pierce," she said tersely, "you'd better come with me. Your sister is awake."

Without a word, Jenny whirled and ran out of the room.

Alex jumped up. "I'm going, too! Even if they don't let me in the room, I can wait outside in the hall."

"We'll all go," Kiki said.

"No! The last thing in the world Julie needs in her room is a crowd." Alex turned to leave. "I'll let you all know how she is, I promise." Then she hurried down to Julie's room.

She had just reached the second floor when she heard the scream.

Chapter 5

Full of anguish, the cry rang out across the white-walled corridor.

Alex ran.

Jenny's voice, frantic and pleading, followed the scream.

The first thing Alex noticed as she burst into the room was the mirror. It was in Julie's left hand, held up in front of her white-cocooned face. The large, oval frame had a long, thick handle fashioned of embellished gold. The intricate design on the handle looked like gold-dipped snakes entwined.

Jenny was trying desperately to wrest the mirror from her sister's grip.

Alex had never seen the twins in even a minor dispute. She was shocked by the sight of the two girls struggling on the bed.

"Give it to me," Jenny sobbed, "please! You're not supposed to have that, not yet.

Where did you get it? Give it to me!"

But Julie, only her eyes and a tiny bit of lip showing through her cocoon of white, clung tenaciously to the ugly mirror handle. Her horrified eyes never left her reflection, and a low, guttural moaning flowed from her lips.

"Where did she get that mirror?" the nurse barked as she rushed into the room. "You give that to me, young lady, this minute!"

She was stronger than Jenny. When she had the mirror safely in hand, she said to Jenny over the sound of Julie's moaning, "Did you give her this?"

Jenny looked at her with stricken eyes. "You think that I — ?"

Alex was livid. She took up Jenny's side. "She would never, *never* do something so cruel," she told the nurse heatedly. "Especially not to her own sister. And she doesn't even own a mirror like that. She'd never buy anything that ugly."

"Well, I'm sorry," the nurse said. "But she's the only person we've allowed in the room. So where did this mirror come from?"

"I didn't," Jenny murmured, "I wouldn't . . ."

"Of course you didn't," Alex soothed. "We know you didn't."

But then, who did? she wondered. Who

would be so cruel? Who wanted Julie to suffer more than she already had?

If I knew who did this, she thought with an anger that surprised her with its ferociousness, I'd . . . I'd . . . Alex took a deep breath. Then she turned to see what the accident had done to Julie.

She couldn't tell. All those bandages . . . the fresh, pretty face was a wad of white, like a snow-covered beehive. But the eyes, from which tears poured, were the same. The same clear blue . . . full, now, of pain and fear.

Alex could only hope that Julie had forgotten she'd ever complained about having a "boring" face. If she remembered, those words would haunt her.

When the nurse had given the distraught patient an injection to calm her down, Alex drew the nurse aside. "Is she going to be okay?"

"Are you a relative?"

"Yes," Alex answered without hesitation. "I'm the older sister."

The nurse eyed her warily, but said after a moment, "It's not as bad as it looks. Her face took quite a beating, but the doctor who was on call is the best. He did some preliminary reconstruction work right away. She'll need more, of course. But at least now she won't look so bad when the bandages come off."

Alex winced. Julie wouldn't look "so bad"? She hoped the nurse wouldn't be tactless enough to use that phrase within Julie's hearing. It would scare her to death.

Julie returned to sleep quickly. Alex was able to persuade Jenny to return to the dorm for a shower and a good night's sleep. They went upstairs to say good-bye to Gabe, and then Marty drove them home.

The sun was shining on the river when they left the hospital. Most of the storm debris had been cleared away. Twin Falls looked normal again. "You'd think the storm had never happened," Alex murmured as they left town.

"But it did," Jenny said, and then fell silent again, staring out the car window.

She must be so scared, Alex thought. Her sister's in the hospital, her parents are so far away. What's it like to be that scared?

I've had it so easy all my life, she told herself, feeling a twinge of guilt. The crash last night is the only bad thing that's ever happened to me. And I wasn't even hurt, not like Julie and Gabe were. And Jenny was hurt, too. Maybe it doesn't show on the outside, but it's there. I can see it in her eyes.

When they got back to campus, Marty went to the library to work on a speech for his sociology class. Jenny took a long, hot shower, while Alex fielded questions about Julie from anxious friends. There was so little she could tell them. Still, they seemed relieved that she had regained consciousness.

"That's a good sign, right?" Finn Conran, a friend of Julie's, asked. "No serious head injury?"

"No, nothing like that. But she'll be in the hospital a while."

That thought was so depressing. Jenny would be over at the hospital most of the time, too. Their dorm room was going to seem so empty.

I'll just go out a lot, Alex decided. I'll visit them at the hospital, and I'll go to football games and to the library and I'll hang out in other people's rooms. Anything to avoid being in our room by myself. Jenny won't be lying on the floor with her glasses on, studying, and Julie won't be sitting on her bed practicing guitar and talking about Gabe or yammering away on the telephone for hours. It won't be the same.

Nothing would ever be the same again.

Still, at least Gabe was going to be able to walk again. The night before, it had looked like maybe he wouldn't be able to. He'd probably even play football again, once his legs had healed.

Maybe Julie would be that lucky, too.

After her shower, Jenny collapsed on her bed and was asleep in minutes.

Alex covered her with a blanket, and then left for her afternoon classes.

She was amazed to find that, except for a few leftover reminders of the storm — broken branches, stray sheets of newspaper clinging to the stadium fence, a cracked window at Dennison Memorial Library — the campus looked the same. Same fountain on the Commons, same Quad — the four buildings joined together —same students hurrying back and forth across campus, same huge old trees and tall metal lampposts lining the campus walkways, same old red brick or buff-colored stone buildings, a few covered with a network of ivy.

Nothing seemed different.

But everything *was* different.

It was just last night, Alex thought in awe . . . just last night that we were in Vinnie's and everything was fine, and I was annoyed that everyone liked that stupid fortune-telling booth, and we ate, and then the storm hit . . .

And everything changed.

After her afternoon classes, Alex had two hours scheduled at WKSM, the campus radio station, where she worked as a DJ. She didn't want to go. What she wanted to do was go home and slide under the covers and sleep until Julie was fully recovered and life was back to the way it had been before the storm.

But if she didn't show up, whoever had the shift ahead of her would be stuck doing double duty. Not fair.

Maybe sitting in the quiet, peaceful booth, taking requests would cheer her up. "I could use cheering up," she murmured, and hurried across campus toward the tower.

Built of buff-colored stone, topped by a set of bells that occasionally played a melody, the tall, narrow tower was twenty stories high. Besides the radio station on the eighteenth floor, it housed offices, a barber shop, the bookstore, a candy shop, and a dry cleaners. A few floors had observation decks equipped with heavy-duty telescopes for studying the heavens.

The office was crowded when she arrived. Kyle was in the soundproof booth, reading sports news. Bennett, back on crutches, and Marty, his nose buried in a stack of papers Alex guessed was the sociology speech, lounged on chairs in the outer office. Jenny, without make-up, her hair yanked away from her face and carelessly fastened with a rubber band, sat behind the station manager's desk.

"You didn't sleep very long," Alex said as she entered the office.

Jenny shrugged. "Couldn't. I came to see if any of these guys wanted to go to the hospital with me. I called, and Julie's allowed to have visitors. She won't want to see everyone, but I'm sure she'd want to see you guys."

The sign on the desk said ROBERT Q PARKER, III, MANAGER, but it lied. Parker had recently been replaced by a cheerful sophomore named Beth Lacey. Alex didn't know much about him, just that he was a "big man on campus," who liked to play around and treated women like dirt. Alex had always avoided him, and she was glad when Beth had taken over. Everyone liked Beth a lot, and the station seemed to be running smoothly under her care.

Marty stood up. "Ready, Jen?"

She nodded, and left the chair.

"Meet us at Vinnie's later?" Marty asked Alex as she opened the door to the booth.

"Oh, pizza again?" Alex groaned. The truth was, she didn't feel up to returning to the place where everything had started, not this soon.

"You can get fettucini Alfredo. You like that better than pizza, anyway. Come on, Alex. I never got a chance to try my fortune last night."

"Well, I'll see."

Alex felt sorry as she watched Bennett hobble off, on crutches. He'd probably done more damage to his knees when he'd tried to help them after the accident. Now, he wouldn't be playing Saturday, after all.

He seemed to be taking it well, though. After all, even with bad knees, he was still better off than Gabe, stuck in a hospital bed.

Saturday's game wasn't going to be much fun. Julie and Gabe wouldn't be there, Bennett wouldn't be playing . . . unless Kyle and Marty got to play more than usual, the whole thing would be a drag.

The others left, and Alex took Kyle's place in the booth. A steady stream of requests kept Alex's mind off Julie and Gabe. She was ten minutes away from the end of her shift when a caller requested a song for Julie Pierce. It was only one of many requests Alex had had for Julie and Gabe.

"Sure," she said, hoping Julie was awake to hear it. "What's the song?"

There was a second or two of silence on the other end of the line, and then a deep, gleeful chuckle. "Play *Who's Sorry Now?*" the voice said in a harsh whisper. "And let us hope she has learned her lesson." The line went dead.

Alex sat perfectly still, her mouth open. She replayed the odd words in her head. Was Julie supposed to be sorry? For what? She hadn't done anything. She'd been the victim of a terrible accident. What was the caller talking about?

Alex didn't play the song. WKSM didn't have it. But even if they had, she wouldn't have played it.

Shaken, she finished her shift, grabbed her jacket, and went to the door to look for her replacement, another freshman named Cath Devon. Cath was the nervous type, always in a rush, sometimes late, but she had a soft, sexy voice that worked well on radio, and she seemed to settle down well once she got inside the booth. Alex couldn't blame Cath for being nervous — after all, she lived in Nightmare Hall.

When Alex checked, Cath wasn't there. There was no one in the outside office.

Darn! She was hungry. She'd eaten no lunch, and only a handful of pecans for breakfast.

She reached down to open the glass-windowed door, but the knob refused to turn. She tried again. Nothing.

Locked? The door to the booth was locked?

Alex groaned. Kyle had accidentally locked the door on his way out? He couldn't have. He wouldn't have been that careless.

Alex struggled with the doorknob for another few minutes. Finally, she gave up and admitted to herself that, carelessness or not, the door was definitely locked.

But . . . how had Kyle managed that? Even if he'd accidentally locked the door, it was the kind of lock that freed itself when the doorknob was turned from the inside. No problem.

Except that when she turned the doorknob, then twisted it harder, nothing happened.

I would call that a problem, Alex thought grimly.

Well, not *that* much of a problem. She was in a radio station, after all, with a telephone right behind her on the console. She would simply call maintenance and have someone come up and get her out. It was only . . . she glanced at the big, round clock on the wall . . . six o'clock. There would be someone in maintenance.

She turned and picked up the telephone that, only minutes ago, had been her link to the outside world. She held the receiver to her ear and had already begun dialing downstairs when she realized there had been no dial tone.

The phone was dead.

Impossible.

She held the receiver out in front of her face and stared at it, as if she expected it to tell her why it had no dial tone.

Then she shook it, and held it to her ear again. The only thing she heard was a maddening silence.

Her mind began dictating to her: Okay, Alex, no need to panic. You are in a radio station booth. All you have to do is put down this stupid, useless telephone, switch on the mike, and announce to all of campus that you are locked in on the eighteenth floor of the tower. Then someone will come and set you free. See? No problem.

And then two things happened.

The lights went out. Without so much as a clicking sound. They went out quietly and quickly and completely, as if electricity suddenly no longer existed.

Alex gasped, and her hand flew up to cover her mouth. Darkness . . . total darkness, had enveloped the booth like a thick black glove.

She could see nothing. Beyond the wide glass doors directly in front of her, leading to the observation deck outside, there was no moon, not even a star shining in the sky.

She made a little sound in her throat. Remember every single thing your mother ever told you about why it was silly to be afraid of the dark, she ordered. Like, there isn't anything in this booth that wasn't here before the lights disappeared. Like, there are no such things as monsters and even if there were, they wouldn't be in this booth with you. Like, darkness is simply the world at rest, getting ready for another day.

But those things hadn't worked well when she was little, and they certainly weren't working now.

This was not supposed to be happening. She had worked in this booth many times, and not once had the electricity gone out, not once had the door locked accidentally, not once had Cath Devon failed to show up at all.

"I am not a little girl anymore," she told the darkness defiantly. "I'm a college freshman, and I'm not afraid of you."

But the darkness knew she lied. She could almost hear it laughing at her.

"I want out of here," she whispered, and suddenly she remembered saying exactly the same thing in the wrecked car the night before.

"Last night was so scary," she whispered. "I don't want something else scary to happen. I'm not ready." And was immediately ashamed for sounding like a small child.

And then the second thing happened.

The double glass doors to the observation deck on the eighteenth floor of the tower blew open and ushered in a wind so strong, it pulled at Alex's hair and whipped against her face and yanked at her clothing and tugged on her legs.

Before she could grab onto the edge of the desk, the wind, a giant vacuum with a strength much greater than her own, yanked her up in its arms and lifted her toward the black, gaping hole beyond the doors.

Chapter 6

Alex struggled to maintain her balance against the vacuuming whirlwind that swept her up and toward the yawning black opening, but it was hopeless. Her feet went out from under her and she landed on the floor on her back, sliding, sliding, swept across the cold tile floor by an unseen hand. Crying out, she flung out her arms, her hands searching desperately for an anchor. But there was nothing . . . nothing. . . .

She had no more breath left in her to scream. Her mouth was open, but only tiny gasps came out.

Cool air slapped against her face as she was cruelly yanked, on her back, across the floor and through the opening, onto the observation deck. The floor was cement, cold and hard. She did cry out, then, as her bruises from the accident bounced against the stone.

Her hands were grasping, searching for something to hold onto . . . something to keep her from going over the edge, eighteen floors above the ground . . . but there wasn't anything, there wasn't anything to grab. . . .

She was sliding across the cement with the speed of a toboggan on ice. Stop, stop, she cried, too fast . . . too fast . . . I can't stop, I can't stop. . . .

Oh, God, she was going to die . . . die . . . smashed to bits on the ground below. . . .

When her searching left hand slapped against something cold and hard, her fingers instinctively wrapped themselves around it. The wind continued to yank at her, nearly pulling her left arm from its socket. But she wouldn't let go. Whatever she had latched onto, it was all she had.

Crying, gasping, clinging with one arm to her anchor, Alex fought to bring her right arm up to join her left. The pain was excruciating. Grunting with the effort, she slapped her right hand around the metal thing and, when that hand met her left one, she laced her fingers together for added strength.

The pull of the angry wind was incredible. Her legs felt as if they were about to be ripped off. She couldn't hold on much longer, and she had no breath left for screaming.

She had forgotten the waist-high wall, built to keep accidents from happening so far above the ground . . . until a sudden, furious gust of wind flung her legs sideways. Had she not been wearing thick socks and boots, both her ankle-bones would have been shattered by the force of the blow as they smashed into the thick stone wall.

She cried out in pain. Then she clenched her teeth and held on. You're not taking me, she vowed grimly. You're not pulling me up and over that wall and tossing me to the ground. I'm never letting go, never!

Her fingers were firmly entwined around the metal . . . pole? . . . She let her head fall to the ground, the cement cool against her cheek, and closed her eyes. But her fingers maintained their steady grip, never easing up for a second.

The wind roared around her, tugging, pulling fiercely . . . but she held on.

And after an eternity, just as Alex was certain she could not hold on another second, the angry wailing suddenly became a moan, and then a sigh, and . . . died.

She was lying in utter, peaceful quiet and the cruel tug at her body was gone.

Unable to move, she lay there, dazed, hands still fastened firmly around the thing that had saved her, her eyes closed.

"Alex? Alex, is that you?"

Beth's voice. Beth would help her. If only Alex could lift her head and ask for help, Beth would give it to her.

"Alex, what on earth . . . ?"

Her head was so heavy. Weighed a ton. Couldn't possibly lift it.

Footsteps rushing across cement. Beth's voice again, "Oh, Alex, what happened?"

"The wind," was all Alex could say.

Arms reaching down to help her up. Trying to unfasten her fingers from around her anchor. "Alex, let go! You have to let go. The wind is gone now, Alex, it's okay."

She had to be told several times before her fingers allowed themselves to uncurl. What she had been holding onto was the base of one of the larger telescopes. It had, she was convinced, saved her life.

"Are you okay?" Beth's soft, gentle voice was saying as she helped Alex back inside to safety. "What on earth happened?"

"I . . . I don't know," Alex answered, collapsing into a chair. "The wind . . ."

"What about the wind?" Beth handed her a glass of water.

"It . . . it pulled the door open, and then it pulled me out . . ." Alex felt silly, although the words were the truth. But they sounded crazy, even to her.

"But you're okay?"

Alex nodded. "Just scared. I really thought I was going to be dragged up and over that wall."

"Gee," Beth said, "I don't remember the wind ever being that rough up here before. Half the time, we don't even close that door. It gets too stuffy in the booth. No one's ever complained about the wind before."

Well, why don't you just *say* I'm nuts and get it over with, Alex thought, annoyed. Aloud, she said, "Thanks for rescuing me. How did you get in? The door to the booth was jammed or something. I couldn't get out."

"Really?" Beth looked even more skeptical. "Actually, it was open a little bit when I got here. I thought that was sort of weird. Where's Cath, anyway?"

"Didn't show."

"Well, that's weird, too. I know she's late sometimes, but she always gets here, sooner or later."

"How could you tell she wasn't here?" Alex asked. "In the dark, I mean?"

"It wasn't dark. The lights were on."

"The lights were on and the door was open?" Alex persisted. "Are you sure?"

"Of course, I'm sure. Alex, what's wrong?" Beth knelt to peer into Alex's face. "I know you must have been scared to death out there. But why are you asking about the lights? And the door? What's been going on here, Alex?"

"The electricity went off," Alex said, rubbing her hands together in an effort to get the circulation going again. Her knuckles were still white. Her fingers throbbed. "And the phone was dead."

Beth stood and picked up the telephone receiver. "It's fine now," she said after a moment. "Listen, you don't look so good. Can you make it back to your dorm okay? Is there someone I can call to come and help you?"

Alex shook her head. She stood up. All she wanted was to get out of this place, as fast as possible. "I'm fine. But . . . but I don't know about tomorrow, Beth. My shift, I mean." She couldn't imagine ever, ever being inside this booth again.

"Don't worry about it. If I don't fire Cath for not showing, she can take your shift. She owes you."

To Alex's amazement, her legs worked. They felt like rubber, and her ankles hurt, but she could walk. Not as fast as she would have liked as she escaped the office, but at least she didn't have to stay there.

She was still too shaken to think about the why and how of what had happened. Later . . . maybe . . . but not now. Now, she needed to be safely back in her room, the lights on, the telephone working.

Shaken to the core, she hoped, prayed, that Jenny would be home. She wanted *someone* there.

Jenny wasn't home.

But the emptiness of the room didn't stop Alex from being glad she was home . . . and safe. She hadn't been thrown eighteen stories to her death . . . not quite. Almost . . .

Almost doesn't count, she thought giddily, and then realized that it certainly did count. Okay, so being dead was the worst. But thinking you were going to be dead was pretty horrible, too.

The thought that she had come close to death two nights in a row was so unbearable, so terrifying, that she swept it out of her head with as much ferocity as any tower wind.

Where had that terrible wind come from? Beth said there'd never been a problem before.

When she had calmed down a little, Alex went to the phone and called first Marty, at his dorm, and then Jenny, at the hospital. Neither was there.

Marty was probably at the library working

on his soc speech. Maybe Jenny had gone down to the hospital cafeteria to get something to eat. Alex tried Kyle and Bennett, also, but no one was home.

Giving up, she decided she really didn't want to talk to anyone, anyway. What would she say? That she'd been dragged to the edge of the observation deck by a gust of wind? How could they possibly understand that?

She didn't understand it herself. If Kyle had accidentally locked the door when he left, how could Beth have found it open? Why was the phone working when Beth picked it up?

She was too tired to think about all of that now. Too tired . . .

She was asleep in minutes, huddled deep within her blankets. She left both lights in her room on, and a third light in the tiny bathroom.

The next day, Alex decided not to tell anyone what had happened on the observation deck. She was beginning to feel foolish about it. According to Beth, no one else had ever had a problem up there in the booth.

She could only hope Beth wouldn't tell anyone what had happened.

In an effort to put the nightmare behind her, Alex agreed to go to Vinnie's that evening after they saw Julie at the hospital. She couldn't stay

65

away from the pizza place forever, just because of a storm, a bolt of lightning, and an auto accident. Anyway, it wasn't Vinnie's fault they'd had a wreck.

Julie, her face still swathed in white, was in better spirits, and making more attempts to talk. They could all see that it was painful for her, but they were so glad to hear her voice, no one told her to quit trying. "At least I can watch television," she told them that night. "And," with a trace of her old impishness, "I'm watching a series on Mystery Theater. It's on every night and I knew by the second episode that the butler didn't do it. The stepdaughter did. She's the only one with motive and opportunity. I'm right, I know I am."

It was wonderful to hear her joking.

She did fall silent when she learned that Gabe was leaving the hospital the following day, on crutches. "I'll miss him," she said after a minute. "He's been keeping me company. But there's no reason for him to stay here. And," she added in a more cheerful tone, "he said he'd come see me a lot."

"Well, good," Jenny said, "because I'm going to have to cut back on my visiting time. I hate to, but I'm getting so far behind in my work, Jules. I'll still come, but — "

"No problem," Julie said hastily. "You were

practically becoming a live-in resident here. Anyway, I can't have company during Mystery Theater, too distracting." She laughed.

But Alex thought the laugh sounded hollow. Maybe it was because of the bandages.

"So, you won't mind if I go to the game Saturday?" Jenny asked her sister.

"No, of course not. Don't be silly. I want you to go. At least there'll be one Pierce twin cheering for the team. Gabe won't be playing, but I know he'll be there. I'll tell him to look for you, Jenny. And Bennett might be playing."

"No way," Marty corrected. "He was on crutches again yesterday."

"Oh. Well, maybe next week. Anyway, you all have to cheer twice as loud to make up for me not being there, okay?"

Alex hated to leave. She had a feeling Julie felt much worse about being left in the hospital — especially now that Gabe was discharged — than she was letting on.

I would, too, if I were in her place, she thought, and gave Julie an extra hug before they all left the room and headed for Vinnie's.

Vinnie's was crowded. The lightning hadn't scared anyone away. Maybe because they've all heard that lightning never strikes in the same place twice, Alex thought as they entered.

Kyle, Kiki, and Bennett were already seated. Much too close to The Wizard to suit Alex. They were right around the corner from it. She couldn't see those creepy blue eyes on her while she ate, but she could feel them. She said nothing to anyone about her feelings. They all already knew, thanks to Jenny, that Alex needed a nightlight to sleep. Admitting that a stupid plaster statue made the hair on the back of her neck stand on end would convince them she should still be in a playpen. Or have her head examined.

Kyle seemed restless. "I don't know why we always come here," he complained. "The pizza isn't all that great, and it's so noisy I can't hear myself think. Why can't we go someplace quiet, for once?"

Alex glanced over at him. What was it that Kyle had on his mind, that he needed peace and quiet to think about? Was he remembering that he'd accidentally locked her in the booth last night? Maybe he was wondering if anything had happened because of his carelessness? Worried that Beth had found out and he was about to be fired?

"Oh, Kyle," Kiki said coyly, "are you worried about the game Saturday? I heard State doesn't have such a great team this year."

Marty laughed. "Kiki, Kyle and I probably

won't even get in the game. Why would he be worried about it?"

Bennett said nothing. Alex felt sorry for him. It must be hard, when he wanted to play so bad, to already know that he had no chance at all.

Bennett said then, "We'll all be there, whether we're playing or not. It's still our team."

Marty and Kyle nodded solemn agreement.

When their food came, Alex noted with amusement that Kiki ate more pizza than anyone else at the table. No diet yet, apparently.

So she was surprised to notice, as they prepared to leave, that Kiki's belt was loose.

"Kiki," she pointed out quietly, "I think your belt's broken."

Kiki looked down. "No, it's not."

"But . . ."

Kiki fumbled with the buckle, adjusted the belt, and slipped into her red ski jacket. "I played four games of soccer this week, Alex. I've probably lost a few pounds, after all that racing around out on the field. It's great exercise."

Before they left, Marty insisted on seeking his fortune at the booth.

Alex tried to talk him out of it. "When you put a quarter in, The Wizard's eyes light up," she argued. "I hate that! It's so creepy!" They were standing directly in front of the booth, and everything Alex had thought earlier about the figure being harmlessly ugly had disappeared from her mind, now that she was facing him. He really was creepy. "Anyway, it's such a waste of money, Marty. Let's just go."

"C'mon — maybe this old codger can tell me how I'm going to fare with my soc speech. I wish I could get out of giving it. I'd rather do anything! Besides, what else can I buy for a quarter these days?"

He dropped the coin in the slot. When he picked up the small white card, he laughed. Holding it out to Alex, he said, "I guess you were right. Waste of money. I think this one was meant for Kyle."

Alex looked down at the card he handed her and read, SILENCE IS GOLDEN. She groaned. "Another old bromide. I swear, my grandmother wrote every single one of these. And you're right. Kyle was the one who wanted peace and quiet. I hate to say I told you so, but you have it coming, so . . . I told you so!"

On their way out of the restaurant, Marty tossed the little white card in the trash.

Chapter 7

Cath Devon called Alex the following morning. "I wanted you to know why I didn't show up," she said anxiously. "I got a call telling me I didn't need to come to the station, that you wanted to work a double shift. I thought that was kind of weird, but the guy who called seemed so . . . definite."

"Who called you?" a half-asleep Alex asked.

"Well, the guy said he was Kyle. It didn't really sound like him, but I've never talked to Kyle on the telephone before, so I don't know."

Alex struggled to clear her mind of the last remnants of sleep. Someone had called Cath and told her not to show up? Why would someone do that?

"Anyway," Cath said, "I'm really sorry. I know I'm late sometimes, but I'd never just not show up, Alex."

"I know that, Cath. And it's okay. Not your

fault. But . . . if it wasn't Kyle, do you . . . do you have any idea who it was that called? I mean, did the voice sound like anyone you knew?"

"I've thought about that ever since Beth told me the call wasn't for real, that it was probably a prank. And no, I didn't recognize the voice, Alex. I'm sorry. I think now whoever was calling was deliberately trying to disguise his voice. With a tissue or something, like in the movies."

When Alex didn't say anything, Cath added, "Beth said you're quitting. It's not because of me, is it?"

"No, Cath, of course not." Alex couldn't bring herself to tell Cath about what had happened out on the deck. But she did ask, "Cath, has the wind off the observation deck ever bothered you at all?"

"The wind? Uh-uh."

Darn.

"Beth probably told you we keep the doors open a lot because the booth gets so stuffy. But I don't remember the wind ever getting nasty, Alex. Is that what happened?"

Beth hadn't told her. Well, good. If Beth hadn't, Alex certainly wasn't going to. "I'm not sure *what* happened, Cath. Anyway, I'm fine now."

"Alex, I really am sorry."

"It's okay, Cath. Thanks."

When Alex had hung up, she sat down on her bed and thought about that observation deck outside the booth.

The radio station wasn't the only thing on the eighteenth floor. There were other offices up there. And that deck went all the way around the building. The offices flanking the radio station must have been empty when she was being torn from the booth and bounced around the deck. Or someone in one of those offices would have heard her scream.

She had screamed, hadn't she? She couldn't remember. Maybe not. Maybe all anyone would have heard was that eerily whistling wind.

Shoving all thoughts of her terror from her mind, Alex got dressed and went to class.

That Saturday provided perfect weather for the football game: brisk, but not really cold, sunny with a clear, blue sky, and only the faintest of breezes.

The stadium was nearly full when Alex, Jenny, and Kiki arrived. Jenny had surprised Alex by putting on makeup, something she'd never done before, and curling her hair before leaving their room. Alex had to admit the effect was stunning. The hair that had always hung, straight, around her shoulders, was now a thick froth of curls that Jenny seemed to take delight in swinging and shaking, the way a woman with a new diamond ring waves her hand about frequently. In place of her customary jeans and sweatshirt, Jenny had dressed in a pair of Julie's black leather pants and a thick peach-colored sweater.

"I'm just trying to cheer myself up," Jenny said when she saw Alex's mouth hanging open in shock. "Wearing Jules's clothes makes me feel closer to her. And besides, she won't mind if I wear them."

Because Alex knew that was true, she said only, "You look really pretty."

Jenny flushed with pleasure. And fastened a pair of Julie's black onyx earrings in her earlobes.

They sat four rows up in the bleachers, directly behind the team bench, at Jenny's insistence. "I want the guys to know we're here, whether they get to play or not."

Alex couldn't argue with that.

She wasn't that wild about the game itself. Too violent. She liked tennis and swimming and basketball, but football broke too many bones. What she did like about football was the atmosphere. Sitting in the stands, even when it was very, very cold and maybe even snowing, friends all around her, all of them there to cheer on their team. Drinking hot chocolate or cider, munching on hot dogs and chips, screaming at the top of her lungs, those were the things that brought her to the stadium. And if she held her breath during a particularly rough play, hoping like mad that no one would break an arm or a leg, she kept that fear to herself.

Milo Keith, Ian Banion, and Jessica Vogt, some other Nightingale Hall residents, were sitting right behind her. Milo was quiet, but he had a wicked sense of humor. Alex sat in front of him in English class, and occasionally laughed aloud at some of the remarks he made about their teacher, Professor Landis.

"I heard Bennett Stark might play today," he said now.

"No way," Ian replied. "I'd heard he might be playing, too, but I saw him before the game and he said he wasn't ready yet. Seemed okay about it, though."

Gabe, of course, wasn't playing, either. But he was sitting on the bench with the team, his crutches propped up beside him.

At halftime, Alex was about to join the long line at the restroom when a voice over the loud-speaker announced, "Telephone for Alexandria Edgar. Telephone for Alexandria Edgar."

Her first thought was *Julie*. Something's happened to Julie. She's worse . . .

She would have run to the nearest phone, but running was impossible in the throng making its way up the stadium steps. She pushed, crying out, "Excuse me, excuse me," but couldn't make herself heard over the noisy crowd. Finally, by leaving the steps and climbing over empty seats, she made her way to the upper deck of the stadium. That, too, was crowded, and no one seemed to know where the nearest phone was located.

Alex pushed and shoved her way through the long lines gathered at the refreshment stands, unable to get close enough to any vendor to ask for directions to a phone. Her name being repeated over the loudspeaker was maddening.

"I know, I know," she muttered, "I hear you . . . I'm trying, I'm trying!"

Finally, a uniformed security guard pointed in response to her question, and she raced around a corner and grabbed the receiver off a black wall phone hidden in an alcove.

"This is Alex Edgar," she cried into the mouthpiece. "I have a phone call?"

A woman's voice said, "Right. Hold on."

Expecting momentarily to hear Julie's voice, Alex's jaw dropped when instead, a deep, unfamiliar voice said in a dull monotone, without so much as a hello, "Hear me well, Alexandria. Are you listening?"

Stupified, Alex stared at the stone wall in front of her. "What?"

"Hear me well. Take me seriously, Alexandria, or you will regret it."

No one called her Alexandria. No one. "Who is this?"

"Do not dispute the wisdom of the ages. Skepticism is dangerous. Heed me well."

There was a click, and the dial tone sounded in Alex's ear.

Slowly, Alex replaced the receiver. Weird. Who . . . ?

She turned away from the phone and walked back around the corner. The crowd had thinned. She could hear the last faint notes of the band's halftime show fading away. The game would be resuming. Time to get back to her seat. Time to watch the rest of the game . . .

If she could put the bizarre phone call out of her mind.

Alex moved slowly, thoughtfully, lost in a fog of confusion. She hadn't recognized the voice. But it could have been disguised. Hadn't it sounded a little like the voice at the radio station, the voice that had requested *Who's Sorry Now* for Julie? She couldn't be sure.

She'd been so surprised to hear a voice that wasn't Julie's that she hadn't been paying enough attention to what the voice did sound like. She had focused only on the words.

Who was it that she wasn't taking seriously?

Alex had a terrible time concentrating on the game. She kept hearing the deep, flat voice ordering her to "hear me well."

Where had it come from?

Salem won the game, but Marty and Kyle were given no playing time. They warmed the bench throughout the game.

Alex knew Marty would be disappointed. But he seemed to be taking it well when they met outside the stadium after the game.

"I hate not being in on a win," Bennett said crankily. "I could have played . . ."

"Stark," Marty said amiably, "do you have any idea how weird that looks, a guy on crutches complaining because he didn't get to play?"

"I meant, if it hadn't been for my knees, I could have played," Bennett said sullenly. "Maybe next week . . ." his voice was wistful.

"Sure. Now, can we just go eat? Sitting on the bench for a couple of hours sure works up an appetite."

No one noticed that Alex was preoccupied. She walked along with the others as they left the stadium for the parking lot, but her mind was elsewhere. Should she tell them about the phone call? Yeah . . . no . . . maybe . . .

What brought Alex back to reality was the surprising but indisputable fact that Jenny was flirting with Bennett.

Flirting? Jenny?

Bennett had, until recently, been dating a gorgeous, red-haired Omega Phi. She'd dropped him like a hot potato the minute he'd taken to crutches. If he wasn't going to be a football hero, she was no longer interested.

Her loss.

Jenny would never be that shallow.

At Alex's insistence, they tried Burgers Etc., a diner not far from school, after the game. But they couldn't even get into the parking lot.

"I don't see why you guys had to take showers," Kiki complained as they drove around the parking lot searching for a space. "You didn't even play!"

"Thanks for pointing that out, Kiki," Marty said drily. "You thought maybe we hadn't noticed that?"

"Well, it let everybody else get here ahead of us. And I'm so hungry I could eat a cow."

Alex had thought that Kiki looked a little thinner when they'd first met in the stands.

Then she'd watched Kiki do nothing but eat chips and pickles and hot dogs and cookies and candy throughout the game and decided she was wrong. No dieting being done here, she'd thought, and helped herself to the bag of cookies sitting on Kiki's lap.

Kyle refused to go to Vinnie's. "It'll be a madhouse. I need peace and quiet, okay? How about Chinese?"

So, they drove into town and ate at Hunan Manor. It was quiet, just as Kyle wanted, and not crowded. At Jenny's gentle coaxing, Bennett finally pulled out of his funk, and they had a good time.

But on the way home, Marty, Bennett, and Kiki insisted on stopping at Vinnie's. "I have to check with The Wizard," Bennett said, half-jokingly. "Maybe he can tell me if I'm going to be able to play next week."

Alex had no intention of going into Vinnie's. "I'll ride back to campus with Kyle," she said as she got out of the car. "Jenny? You said you were tired."

"I am." Jenny hesitated, then smiled at Bennett. "But I think I'll stay."

They all argued with Alex, especially Jenny. "Why go back to the room and be alone? C'mon, Alex, we won today, and we haven't really celebrated."

But Alex wasn't in any mood for celebrating. She could have told them about the phone call, but she was afraid they'd think she was being silly. Marty would say it was obviously just a joke. They'd think she was making too much of it.

Maybe she was.

"C'mon," Bennett urged, "you haven't had your fortune told yet. Now's your chance."

"I don't want my fortune told," Alex said sharply. "That stupid Wizard is totally bogus, and you all know it. I wouldn't waste my money on that thing."

Surprised by her reaction, they all began backing away. "Alex, chill," Kyle chided. "He might hear you."

"Who?"

Kyle laughed. "The Wizard, dummy. He could have far-reaching powers, Alex. You wouldn't want to hurt his feelings, would you?"

"He's right," Kiki said, grinning. "You should watch what you say about someone who has the power to grant wishes and tell fortunes, Alex. You could be asking for trouble."

Alex regarded both of them with suspicion. "Did either of you make any phone calls during halftime?"

Kyle looked bewildered. "Phone calls?"

But Kiki's grin widened. "Why?" she asked

with phony innocence. "Did you get one? Did you, for instance," her words deliberately slow and measured, "get one from someone who warned you about being skeptical?" And then she cleared her throat, and with one hand over her mouth, repeated in a low monotone the words Alex had heard over the phone. "Hear me well, Alexandria, skepticism can be dangerous." Laughing, Kiki pointed at Alex's face. "You should see yourself! I wish I had a camera."

"You made that stupid call?" Alex's face burned. "It was you?"

"Oh, relax, Alex. I was just having fun. You were such a drag about The Wizard. Where's your sense of humor?"

"Maybe I left it in Julie's backseat the night of the accident," Alex snapped. Lips clamped together, she whirled in disgust and walked stiffly to the edge of the parking lot to await the shuttle.

There was whispering and muttering behind her, and then Marty was standing beside her. "I sent everyone else on inside," he said. "What's up? What was that all about?"

"I actually thought, for just one tiny little second, that it might be him," she murmured, so low that Marty couldn't hear her. And it's not really Kiki I'm mad at, she thought angrily, it's myself. For being so incredibly stupid.

Marty bent his head toward hers. "What? What are you mumbling about?"

Alex shook her head. "Nothing. Never mind." She felt like such a fool.

He was annoyed with her lack of response. "Why are you pooping out on us? C'mon inside, Alex. It's too early to call it a night."

"I don't want to go in there," she said. "Like Kyle said, it's too noisy. I have a headache."

"You've always liked Vinnie's," Marty said, a frown furrowing his forehead. "What's up?"

What was up was that being in Vinnie's reminded her of the storm and the lightning and the accident. She didn't want to be reminded of any of those things. And then there was that stupid wooden Wizard, fixing his cold blue eyes on her as if he could see right through her. Reminding her of what a fool she was, not guessing that Kiki was behind the stupid practical joke.

Maybe dieting made Kiki irrational. Because in spite of the enormous amount of food she'd eaten tonight, she really did look thinner.

"I told you, I'm tired," Alex repeated, becoming as annoyed as he was. "I mean, I don't have to do everything everyone else does, do I? I want to go home, and that's what I'm going to do, okay?"

"Okay, okay! Forget I said anything. See you!" And he turned on his heel and walked, head down, back to the restaurant and went inside.

Good. Who needed him? He could never understand how foolish she felt.

Because she had thought, just for that tiny, awful little second, that The Wizard had actually called to warn her not to doubt him.

Chapter 8

When Alex got back to the dorm, the sounds of some heavy-duty partying echoed from one of the rooms on her floor as she entered the hall.

The temptation to join the party was strong. Tired or not, she hated the thought of going back to an empty room again. All she had to do was knock on the door, and she'd be with other people. Maybe even having fun, who knew? She could forget about Julie's face and Gabe's injured legs and Marty being annoyed with her. She could push everything, including her battle with the tower wind, out of her mind, just for a little while, and have a good time. Wasn't that what parties were for?

Alex hesitated in the hallway. If Marty found out she'd refused to stop at Vinnie's with them and then had gone to a party instead, he'd be double-ticked.

Too bad. She hadn't said she wanted to go home and go to bed. She'd only said she didn't want to go into Vinnie's. And that was the truth.

Alex marched straight over to the source of the party sounds and rapped sharply on the door.

It was opened by a short, pretty girl with blonde hair. Alex had seen her at parties. She was a friend of the Omega Phi redhead who'd been dating Bennett. The blonde girl's name, Alex remembered, was Amber.

She let Alex in and handed her a brimming paper cup. "You're Alex Edgar," she said. "Aren't you a friend of Bennett's?"

Alex nodded. The room was thick with people, lounging, sitting. There didn't seem to be a square inch of empty space.

"Poor Bennett," Amber said. "He was really nuts about Shelley. But she doesn't date non-athletes. Ever. I guess Bennett was really wrecked over it."

"Doesn't seem to be," Alex said coolly. If Bennett was wrecked, she was positive he wouldn't want Shelley and all of her friends to know it. "He was having fun tonight with Jenny Pierce."

"Oh, the twin of that girl whose face was totalled."

Alex winced at the remark. Turning away, she stepped carefully around reclining bodies sharing a huge bowl of pink popcorn, and went to the window. Squeezing between two people she didn't know, she made a space for herself and stood looking out. The tower was directly across from her.

"Hey, Alex!" a girl named Jill from Alex's math class called out, "You're being antisocial. How's Julie doing?"

Alex turned around and joined in the conversation and, after a while, the fun. When she next turned back to the window, she was surprised to see people on the sixth floor observation deck of the tower. They were directly in her line of vision. Two figures, moving about. Dancing? Maybe they'd taken a tape player up there and were dancing under the stars. How romantic. Cold, even without the wind, but romantic.

She couldn't see who the couple was. Too far away, and the lights on the deck weren't that bright. They wouldn't be looking at the stars. If they were going to do that, they'd have gone higher up, maybe even to the eighteenth floor, where the bigger telescope was . . . the one that had saved her life.

One of the figures moved away from the

other, waving its arms. It didn't seem that they were dancing anymore.

Alex peered through the glass, ignoring the laughter and loud conversation behind her. There was something about the taller of the two figures . . . something familiar. The height? The build? The way it moved around the deck? Something. . . .

Suddenly the shorter figure began to back away, slowly at first, his or her head turning from side to side as if looking for something. Then he began running from one side of the stone wall to the other, while the taller one remained in place with his back to the door leading from the tower.

Blocking it, Alex thought all of a sudden. The door is being blocked so the shorter one can't get to it.

Why?

It looks like the shorter person is trying to run away, Alex thought, and realized instantly that that was exactly what was happening. The figure dashing frantically about on the observation deck was running from the taller one, who was blocking the only escape route.

But there's nowhere to go, she thought next, leaning closer against the window. Her forehead gently bumped the glass. It felt cool, refreshing in such a hot, stuffy room. Why does he need to get away? The other person isn't doing a thing . . . just standing there. Nothing scary about that.

So why was the other person running frantically around on the observation deck like a rat caught in a maze?

The taller figure began to move . . . slowly . . . toward the shorter one, who was rapidly backing up against the waist-high wall. When his back had collided with the stone and he could no longer move, his hands moved up and out, in a defensive posture. As if he knew a fight was coming.

Alex stood up straighter. What was going on? They definitely weren't dancing, and they weren't being romantic . . . were they just fooling around?

Alex didn't know what to do. Call security? What if it was just two people horsing around? She'd feel like an idiot. And the two people, whoever they were, not to mention the security guard, would think she had nothing better to do than stand at a window and spy on other people.

But what if they weren't just horsing around?

The shorter person now stood with his back against the stone wall, hands raised, as the taller person approached. There was something very odd about the figure, something Alex couldn't place . . . what *was* it?

He looks like he's laughing, Alex thought, and felt an enormous sense of relief. If he was laughing, there couldn't really be anything wrong, could there? She'd been right not to race to the phone and call security. They were playing.

And then, with Alex still watching, the approaching figure reached the wall. His arms reached out, made contact, and, for a moment, seemed to be toying with the other person's shirt.

Alex heard Jill calling to her and she flushed in embarrassment. She felt like a Peeping Tom.

And then, just as she was about to turn away from the window in disgust with herself, the taller figure lifted the other one and threw him up and over the side of the observation deck.

Chapter 9

Alex screamed. The sound went unheard in a room raucous with music and laughter.

The figure that had been thrown off the deck arched up, up, and out into the air before beginning his rapid spiral downward. Arms and legs flailed wildly, grasping outward for something to stop his flight. Alex could feel his mouth opening, could hear, in her mind, his futile screams for help, help, *help*. . . .

The figure slammed into the awning over the second floor deck and bounced off, arching up again before he made his final descent.

The arms and legs no longer flailed.

In her mind, Alex heard the awful thud when the figure slammed into the ground.

Then he lay still, arms and legs sprawled awkwardly.

People who had been walking across campus began running toward the unmoving figure.

Alex, so ill she could barely stand, sagged against the window. "Someone," she whispered, "someone was thrown off the tower."

No one heard her.

She took a deep, cleansing breath and whirled away from the window. No one was paying any attention. People were rummaging through a pile of CD's in one corner of the room and people in the middle of the room were making a futile attempt to dance, and other people were lying on the floor tossing popcorn at each other, but no one was paying any attention to the fact that someone had just been thrown off the sixth-floor observation deck of the tower.

"Someone *fell!*" she screamed, and this time everyone stopped what they were doing and looked. "From the tower! Call an ambulance! Hurry!"

Then, as someone reached for the phone, Alex stumbled through the crowd to the door and ran out of the room.

Followed by Amber and Jill, Alex raced out of the building and to the tower.

A crowd had already gathered. Alex, her breath coming in ragged gasps, pushed her way through it. And saw Marty, kneeling on the ground beside . . . Kyle!

It was Kyle she had watched go off that tower. Kyle . . .

He was lying on his back, a spreading puddle of red covering the grass underneath his blond hair. He wasn't moving, but . . . Alex's eyes moved quickly to his chest . . . he was breathing.

Her knees gave, and she sank to the ground, close to Marty.

"He's not dead," Marty said quickly. He looked up, glancing around the crowd, and repeated, "He's not dead." Bennett and Gabe, who were close by, nodded. Jenny and Kiki, their faces a sickly yellow in the tower lights, stood next to them, crying, their hands over their mouths.

"Did he jump?" a voice in the crowd asked.

"No!" Alex cried, furious. "He didn't!" She would have added then, "He was thrown over the side." But even as someone said casually, "Well, people *have* jumped from there, you know," sirens screamed, and Alex got to her feet. There was something she had to do.

Without a word to anyone, she turned and pushed back through the crowd, ignoring Marty's shocked, "Alex? Where — ?"

She ran to the tower entrance, praying it wouldn't be locked.

It wasn't. Yanking the heavy door open, she went inside and ran straight to the stairs. No time to wait for the elevator to the sixth floor.

If the police came with the ambulance, as they probably would, they wouldn't let anyone into the tower until they'd checked it out. They wouldn't let her up there. And she had to see the place Kyle had fallen from, see it for herself, see if there was anything to tell her who had done this terrible thing.

The tower was deserted. It was late. The staircase was dimly lit, by only one small light at the top of each flight of stairs. Hardly enough to see by. It was cold in the stairwell, and silent. Her footsteps echoed so loudly on the stone steps, she was sure the people outside would hear and come to see what she was up to.

Third floor . . . fourth floor . . . out of breath . . . keep going . . . have to see if Kyle's attacker left anything, anything at all . . .

Fifth floor, one more flight . . . ah! the door to the sixth floor.

She hesitated. He wouldn't still be around, would he . . . Kyle's attacker?

No. He would have left the moment he saw the crowd gathering. No one who had done what he'd done would hang around, waiting to be caught.

Alex hurried on.

So dark . . . no one around. Security guards? Where would they be? If they found her, they'd stop her. Maybe they'd even think she was somehow involved.

But they'd probably heard Kyle's screams and had rushed outside. They'd be out there now, wanting to help.

Could anyone help Kyle now? There was . . . so much blood under his head and he lay there so quietly, so quietly. . . .

Alex ran down the hall, searching for the entrance to the observation deck on the side facing Lester. Offices, offices, all empty now, all dark. The clickety-clack of her boot heels on the polished wood floor hurt her ears. She smelled cleaning fluid . . . where was the cleaning staff? On another floor?

Here! Here was the door she wanted. She pulled it open cautiously, in case she'd been wrong about Kyle's attacker leaving, and was immediately assaulted by a gust of wind ripping at her face and hair.

But it died quickly, unlike the vicious evening wind up on the eighteenth floor.

There was no one on the deck. Nothing but a few tall potted plants.

Alex tried to think, to concentrate, as the heavy door slammed shut behind her. Where had the two figures been standing? She couldn't remember. Think, think, think. . . .

She ran to the edge of the wall and cautiously

peered down. The crowd looked like miniature people, so far below her. A circling blue light on top of one vehicle below her, a similar light, this one red, on a larger vehicle. Police and ambulance. The police would be in the tower at any moment.

She turned to face the deck, and felt sick again. Why would someone throw sweet Kyle to his death? Kyle had never hurt anyone. He couldn't. It wasn't in him. On the football field, maybe, but nowhere else.

And it *was* death that Kyle's attacker had intended. No question about that. You didn't toss a person from a sixth story and expect him to get up and walk away with a few harmless bruises and maybe a scrape or two.

Conscious of each passing minute, Alex scoured every inch of the stone deck, aided only by yellow lights on the deck roof.

Nothing. She found nothing.

Remembering what she had witnessed, replaying it in her mind, she tried to follow every step that Kyle and his enemy had taken.

Still finding nothing, she stopped and leaned against the wall, beside a tall potted plant, its fernlike branches swaying in the wind. One soft, delicate branch brushed against her cheek. She slapped it away impatiently.

A departing siren's wail told her time was

running out. Kyle was on his way to the hospital. The police would be on their way up here. They'd make her leave the deck, and she hadn't found a thing that would help identify the person who had hurt Kyle.

The feathery branch tickled her cheek again. Frustrated by her disappointing search, she swatted at the greenery so hard the stem broke and fell into the base with a faint whooshing sound.

Alex's eyes guiltily followed its descent. And saw, at the base of the plant, something gleaming in the weak yellow lights. Something small . . . and golden.

She reached down and picked it up.

A tiny, gold football, with a small golden hoop in the center so that it could be worn on a chain.

Alex stared at the tiny charm, rolling it in the palm of her hand. How long had it been hiding in the pot? It wasn't dirty. Couldn't have been in there very long.

Of course, anyone could have dropped it. Anyone. At any time. Not necessarily on this particular Saturday night.

Or . . . Kyle himself could have lost it, when he was racing back and forth on the deck, trying to find a way out.

Imagining how frightened he must have

been, Alex closed her eyes in pain. He must have known something terrible was about to happen to him, or he wouldn't have been moving so frantically. But he couldn't possibly have imagined *how* terrible, could he?

Just then, a security guard arrived, followed by two Twin Falls policemen in uniform. They immediately demanded to know what she was doing on the deck.

She told them. She told them everything she'd seen. Then she gave them the football charm, telling them where she'd found it. One of the policemen took it from her and dropped it into a plastic bag he took from his pocket.

"It wasn't an accident?" he said. "You actually saw someone throw the victim off this deck? Are you sure? Where were you at the time?"

"I'm positive." Alex pointed to Lester. "I was over there. At a party. In that room with all the lights on." She could see people moving around in Amber's room. The light over there was much brighter than the deck lighting.

"Anyone know you saw this?" the policeman asked her in a casual voice.

"Oh, sure," Alex said, thinking at first that he wanted to corroborate her story. "Everyone who was at the party knows I saw it happen."

"Hmm. Might want to tell them to keep it

to themselves," he said in that same casual tone, and his partner nodded emphatically.

And then Alex got it. Her stomach rose up to meet her throat. Oh, God, she'd been a witness to a crime, and everyone at the party knew it! They'd tell other people, and those people would tell more people, and soon everyone on campus would know that she'd seen what happened to Kyle. Including . . .

Including the person who had committed the crime.

"Which window, exactly, was it?" the policeman asked her. "Where you were standing, I mean. Can you point it out?"

"Yes. The party's still going on." Amber's guests hadn't been as rattled by Kyle's tragedy as Alex had. She led the two policemen to the edge of the deck and pointed out the window. As they watched, a girl came to the window and looked down upon the Commons, perhaps checking to see if things had returned to normal.

Alex could see her clearly. Long, blonde hair, a green shirt . . . it was Amber. And if *Amber* was identifiable from the sixth floor deck . . .

Alex gasped in horror.

Chapter 10

It was a stricken Alex who finally breathed in disbelief, "But I can see Amber from here! I can even tell what color her hair is!" She turned toward the officers. "I couldn't see who was over *here*. It never occurred to me that anyone could have seen *me*!"

"Lighting's better over there," the older policeman said.

Alex took a shaky step backward. "But . . . but that means . . . that means he saw me *watching*! And," she ran a hand through her shoulder-length dark hair, "I've got this white streak in my hair, I've had it forever, no one else on campus has it, if he could see *that*, he . . . he . . ."

"You don't know that he saw you at all," the policeman said. "The way you told it, his attention was pretty much focused on the victim. He'd have had to turn and look sideways, at that building, to see you standing there. Did you see him do that at any time?"

Alex thought for a minute. No, she didn't think he had turned. Wouldn't she remember if he had turned and looked at her? The thought gave her chills.

"We'll check out the party guests," she was told, "tell them mum's the word about what you saw. And you keep it to yourself, understand? Until we know more, I would suggest you tell no one. *No one.*"

Alex nodded silently.

The policemen walked her back to her dorm. On the sixth floor, she pointed out Amber's room, and they left in search of party guests.

But first, they told her to lock her door.

She locked it with shaking hands.

There was a note from Jenny on the bathroom mirror. She had gone to the hospital, with Marty, Bennett, Gabe, and Kiki, to find out how Kyle was.

Alex went to the phone.

The nurse who answered would tell her only, "Mr. Leavitt is resting comfortably."

Resting comfortably? What did that mean?

Well, it meant Kyle wasn't dead. That was enough for now.

She was too tired to wait up for Jenny. Sleep . . . she needed sleep . . .

She fell into bed with her clothes on, and was asleep in minutes.

But she did not rest comfortably. Her subconscious served up a smorgasbord of horrifying images that caused Alex to thrash and moan all night long. First she saw Julie, from the back: thick, short hair shining like gold, free of bandages. Then she turned around . . . and she had no face. There was only an empty oval where her features should have been. It was like looking into a mirror with no glass, and Alex, in sleep, saw again the grotesque mirror the twins had wrestled over in the hospital. In her dream, she began hunting for the ugly thing, searching the hospital room, looking in the closet and in the bathroom. There was no sign of it, and no clue about where it had come from.

Then the nightmare scene changed and she was standing in the doorway of another room, a small, cold, white cubicle, with only a white table inside. A figure lay on the table, covered to its neck with a heavy black cloth. Alex didn't want to go inside. But she was pulled in by a force stronger than herself. Closer, closer . . . music came from somewhere, slow and haunting, like a funeral dirge. She clapped her hands over her ears, but her legs kept moving closer and closer to the black-draped table. She could see the chin, the nose . . . Kyle! Lying like stone, unmoving, unblinking, his eyes wide open, staring up at her. His skin was gray and looked as cold and smooth as marble.

Then his lips moved, and as she gasped and jumped backward, he said in a hoarse voice, *"Peace and quiet, peace and quiet, I have peace and quiet, Alex."*

Kyle's image was replaced by Gabe's. He was rolling down the hospital corridor on a wheeled cart that sat low to the ground, like a child's go-cart. He had no legs. "Look, Alex," he cried happily, grinning up at her, "I've finally got wheels!" As she stared at him, he raced down the hall and around a corner and disappeared.

And then the face of The Wizard was gazing down at her, his blue eyes glinting, his mouth open beneath the white beard and mustache, and he threw his head back and laughed, ha-hahahahahaha, like the ugly pink woman Alex had hated at the amusement park. *Hahaha-hah . . .*

Alex jerked awake, moaning, covered in a cold sweat.

The phone rang.

It was one of the policemen. "I've done some checking about that football charm you found. They were given to all the freshmen when they made the football team this year. They come with a gold chain. But most of the guys probably put them away somewhere, with their high school class ring."

Freshman football players? There were several freshmen on the team, including Marty, Gabe, and Bennett . . . Shivering, Alex offered, "I could ask around, see who made a practice of wearing theirs or carrying it around with them."

"No!" he said sharply, surprising her. "Don't talk to anyone about this. Let us handle it. And, Miss, I wouldn't go anywhere alone. Keep friends with you or your boyfriend . . ."

She didn't tell him she didn't have a boyfriend.

When Alex hung up, a wave of uneasiness washed over her. Did she really need to keep someone with her at all times, at least until they caught the person who had attacked Kyle? They didn't even know if he had seen her.

He didn't, she told herself as she put on her bathrobe. I know he didn't. I would have seen him looking at me. Wouldn't I?

But she'd been upset, watching. Hadn't she closed her eyes when Kyle fell? He might have looked over at her then.

Maybe? she asked herself cynically as she thrust her telltale white streak of hair up under a green felt hat. Don't you mean probably, almost certainly, what-are-the-chances-that-he-didn't? Isn't *that* what you mean?

Jenny came out of the shower, her hair, untoweled, dripping on the shoulders of her green robe. "You okay?" she asked Alex. "You didn't sleep very well last night. You were fighting with your sheets and making all these weird noises."

"Sorry."

"That's okay. I didn't get in until late, anyway." Jenny moved to the closet to pick out something to wear. "After Bennett and I found out that Kyle wasn't going to wake up at all last night, we went for a drive. We were both pretty upset, and it was a nice night out."

Bennett and I? They were "Bennett and I" now?

"Awful what happened to Kyle, isn't it?" Jenny went on, her voice muted as she rummaged in the depths of the closet. "You don't think he jumped, do you?"

I was wrong, Alex thought, sitting down on the bed. There is at least one person on campus who doesn't know that I saw it happen. So maybe lots of people don't know.

Without waiting for Alex's answer to her question, Jenny continued, "Where did you disappear to, anyway? Marty was really mad that you didn't come to the hospital with us."

But he hadn't come into the tower looking for her, *had* he? Aloud, Alex said, "I had something I had to do. And it's not like I could have helped Kyle. He *is* going to be okay, isn't he?"

"Well, no one knows yet. He's in a coma."

"A coma?" Alex remembered her nightmare . . . Kyle lying still as death, his face as cold and smooth as wax. "Will he be okay?"

"No one knows." Jenny emerged from the closet with a gold silk blouse of Julie's and a pair of black velvet jeans. "And no one really knows what happened. Maybe we'll never know if he jumped or not."

"He wouldn't do that!" Alex snapped. She wanted to tell Jenny the truth, but the cops had been very clear about that. She had to keep quiet about what she'd seen. For now, anyway.

Jenny shrugged. "Kyle was a big football hero in high school, just like Bennett and Marty and Gabe. You know how they talk about football, like it's the most important thing in the world. So did Kyle. He was shattered at not being a hero anymore. Maybe he was more depressed than we realized."

Alex had to bite her tongue to keep from shouting, "He didn't jump! Someone threw him off that tower!" She said instead, "I'm going down to see Kyle. And Julie. You coming?"

"They won't let you see Kyle. And I already told Julie I can't come today. I've . . . I've got stuff I have to do. Research. At the library, with Bennett."

Research? In a gold silk blouse and black velvet jeans?

"I thought you'd be going today. You've hardly seen Julie this week."

"She doesn't mind. She doesn't like people seeing her the way she is now. They took her bandages off, and she's just got these little pieces of tape, and you can see all the stitches . . ." Jenny shuddered. "I don't blame her for not wanting people around. Anyway," she added lightly, "my parents are coming tomorrow. They'll keep her company. They dote on her, you know. Always did."

Jenny began experimenting with hairstyles in front of the mirror, and Alex left to take a shower.

When she came back, Jenny was gone. Her books were lying on her unmade bed.

Research without books? The only research Jenny Pierce was probably going to get done today was an analysis of Bennett Stark, ex-jock.

That was probably why Jenny hadn't seemed devastated over what had happened to Kyle . . . because she was suddenly so wrapped up in Bennett. Maybe falling in love made you forget other people, at least for a while. And it must be nice for Bennett, after not being able to play football and being dumped by that girl, Shelley. At least he had a girlfriend again, one who liked him for himself instead of his letterman's jacket.

Jenny was right about Julie's face. Alex had to struggle to keep from letting a gasp of horror escape when she walked into Julie's room. The swath of white bandages had been replaced by small strips of clear adhesive. Every ugly black stitch, every swollen lump of tissue, every patch of black and purple and yellow showed through.

"I know it looks horrible," Julie said hastily as Alex entered with Kiki, Marty, and Gabe. "I'm sorry. You don't have to stay if you don't want to."

The statement was so unlike her, it startled Alex, snapping her mind away from the damaged face. She sounds so . . . beaten, she thought, and hurried to Julie's bedside. "Don't be silly. We're not going anywhere. We just got here." She sat down on the bed, carefully. "You do look pretty awful, though," she said breezily. "If I were you, I'd ditch whatever makeup you're using. It's not working." And then she held her breath, because if Julie didn't laugh . . .

Julie laughed. And even though she immediately put her hands to her face because the laughter hurt, Alex relaxed a little. As long as Julie could still laugh, she'd be okay.

"Kiki," Julie said then, "are you really dieting this time? You look thinner."

Alex was amazed to notice that Kiki did look thinner. Not thin, but thinner. Her cheekbones were clearly visible. Maybe she'd just found a new way to apply makeup. She's going to be really beautiful if she keeps this up, Alex thought.

But there was no dieting that day. Kiki had something in her mouth every time Alex looked at her. Cookies, chips, nuts, candy . . .

She's going to eat herself right out of those jeans, Alex thought. She noticed that Kiki's leather belt was drooping around her waist, but at the rate she was going, Alex was sure it would be strangling her by mid-afternoon.

"I'm going down to see Kyle," Alex announced. "If they'll let me. I can at least find out how he's doing. Anyone want to come?"

Marty came with her. He didn't talk on the way down to the intensive care unit, and she found herself feeling very uncomfortable. She couldn't remember now exactly why he was mad at her. For leaving the scene last night, that she knew . . . but hadn't there been something before that? She couldn't remember what it was. And she was more concerned about Kyle right now.

They were not allowed to see him. "Only immediate family members," the nurse told them crisply when they arrived.

That sounds familiar, Alex thought, annoyed. "Well, can you at least tell us how he is?"

"The same. No change." And the nurse disappeared into a storage closet.

Alex was about to turn away when she saw an envelope lying on the nurse's desk behind the tall white counter. It was large and brown. Alex could see quite clearly Kyle's name written across the front in black.

She found herself wondering if Kyle's things, the things he'd had on him when he got to the hospital, were in there. Had to be. It was that kind of envelope. His watch, his wallet . . . Why hadn't the police taken the envelope?

Because Kyle hadn't *committed* a crime, he'd been the victim of one. The police had no reason to take his things.

But Alex did. She needed to see if there was something — *anything* — that might help her figure out who had attacked him — and why. She wasn't sure what she was looking for, but she had to see.

"Whàt are you doing?" Marty hissed as Alex darted around the side of the high white counter and stretched out an arm to snatch up the envelope.

"Never mind. Keep an eye out for unexpected company, okay? This'll just take a minute."

While he watched, disbelieving, Alex yanked open the clasp on the envelope and fumbled around inside. Her fingers closed around a small, oval metal object on a chain. She peered inside and saw it was just what she'd thought. A gold football charm.

That meant one thing. The charm she'd found in the plant on the observation deck wasn't Kyle's. He'd been wearing his, and was still wearing it when he was admitted to the hospital's emergency ward the night before.

The one in the plant belonged to someone else.

The question was, Who? And how long, exactly, had that football been sitting in the potted plant on the sixth-floor observation deck of the tower?

Not long, Alex was positive. Not long at all.

Without withdrawing the ornament, she refastened the envelope flap, put the envelope back on the desk, and grabbed Marty's hand. "C'mon, let's go!"

"What was that all about?" he demanded as they ran back up the stairs to Julie's room.

"Something I needed to check out. Tell you later." Changing the subject, she said, "What do you want to bet there isn't a crumb of food left in Julie's room? Kiki seems to be making up for lost time. And I'm getting hungry."

"We go straight to Vinnie's from here," Marty said curtly, and Alex nodded.

When they walked into the room, Gabe was sitting on Julie's bed, giving her a play-by-play of the game the day before, and Kiki was crumpling an empty plastic bag, preparing to toss it into the wastebasket on the opposite side of Julie's bed.

Kiki stood up to throw.

Alex noticed as Kiki left the chair that the brown leather belt seemed to be drooping even more than it had before. Kiki must have loosened it. Couldn't blame her. Those jeans must be getting pretty snug around the waist after all that junk food.

Kiki lifted her arm to aim the crumpled ball of cellophane and stood on tiptoe to throw. Then suddenly, she said in a startled voice, "Oh, wow," and collapsed. Her eyes rolled back in her head, her mouth fell open, her eyes fell shut, and she slid down, landing in a heap on the floor.

Chapter 11

A terrible sense of doom swept over Alex as she saw Kiki collapse. She watched with an odd sense of detachment as Kiki's head hit the floor with a thunk, watched as her arms and legs flopped like the limbs on a rag doll.

Maybe she's dead, she thought dispassionately, suddenly too weary to feel anything.

Alex realized then that she had made a mistake. She had thought that coming to the hospital to visit Julie, which was what you did if you happened to have a friend in the hospital, would make things seem at least a little . . . *normal*. And after everything that had happened lately, normal sounded pretty good.

But it hadn't worked. Because here was Kiki, flopped on the floor with her eyes closed. Kiki might be a little bit different in some ways, but she didn't usually go around fainting.

"You would think," Alex said aloud in a

strange, flat voice, "that a hospital room, of all places, would be *safe*. But I see that it isn't. It just isn't. Maybe no place is."

Gabe and Marty bent to help Kiki. Julie pressed frantically on her call button for a nurse, her bruised eyes regarding Alex with concern. "Alex, what's the matter? She just fainted, I think. Why are you acting so strange?"

Alex turned to face her. "Why am I acting so strange? Why am I acting so *strange*? You're in the hospital and so is Kyle, and Gabe is out of the hospital but he's on crutches, and I . . ." She almost said, "And I saw one of my friends get thrown off a sixth-floor observation deck last night," but she stopped herself in time. She wasn't supposed to tell anyone, she remembered. "How should I act?" Tears gathered in her eyes. "And now here's Kiki, lying on the floor and for all I know, she's dead. I wouldn't be at all surprised."

Kiki wasn't dead.

"She's fainted, that's all," the nurse kneeling by Kiki's side said, looking up at Alex, who was wringing her sweatshirt in her hands. "And I know why, too," the nurse added crisply. "Look at how loose her clothes are." Kiki began to stir. "This girl's been crash-dieting, I guarantee it. I've got a teenaged daughter who doesn't eat enough to keep a bird alive, and I know a starvation dieter when I see one."

"But she's been eating all afternoon!" Alex cried.

"I'm not surprised. And I wouldn't be surprised to hear what she's been eating contained enough sugar to create a vat of cotton candy, am I right? Cookies, candy, cake . . ."

Alex nodded.

Kiki's eyes opened.

"Right," the nurse said. "She's been starving herself, and today she decided to overload her system with sugar. No wonder she hit the floor. When will you girls learn? If you really want to lose weight, you load up on fruits and veggies, some bread, a little chicken, a little fish, and you'll lick the problem for life."

"I hate fish," Kiki murmured.

But she was able to leave the hospital in half an hour. She left accompanied by a stern last-minute lecture from the nurse about "proper eating habits."

"Sorry, guys," Kiki said when they were in the car. "I guess I scared you. Didn't mean to. Especially you, Alex. You look terrible. *You're* not going to faint, too, are you?"

"No. I'm just glad you're okay. I couldn't take one more person being in the hospital."

At least, Kiki hadn't been attacked. Alex

was grateful for that much. Her "accident" had been of her own making. For just one second there, when Kiki first began to crumble, Alex had flashed back to last night and Kyle falling, falling . . .

But he hadn't fallen. He'd been thrown. Big difference. And he'd been thrown, she remembered now, by someone who might have seen her watching. Alex was so thoroughly rattled that she couldn't remember what she had planned to ask Marty. As they drove to Vinnie's, where Kiki promised to order a healthy salad, Alex racked her brain. It had been something important, she remembered that much. Something to do with last night . . .

There were so many questions about last night. Which one had she planned to ask Marty?

Oh, yes. "Marty," she said, turning toward him on the front seat, "when you first made the team, did you get one of those little gold footballs on a chain?"

"Yeah. How'd you know about those?"

Oops. She couldn't tell him. "I saw one somewhere. Can't remember who was wearing it. Anyway, I asked him about it, and he said all the freshman football players got them. So I just wondered. I've never seen you wearing one."

"I had it on my key chain," he said.

Alex glanced at the keys hanging in the ignition. No tiny gold football hung there.

"Lost it," Marty said, seeing her glance. "A while ago. It must have dropped off."

"Where did you lose it?" she couldn't help asking.

He laughed. "You know, Alex, I've always thought that was one of the dumber questions in this world. My mother used to throw that at me all the time. I'd be missing my glasses or my wallet or a book, and she'd always say, 'Well, where did you lose it?' Think about that for a minute, Alex. If I knew where I'd lost it, it wouldn't be lost, would it? I'd *know* where it was, right?"

"Okay, okay, don't get testy. I just meant, do you have any idea where you were when you lost it. And that's probably what your poor mother meant, too, but I suppose you bit her head off like you just did mine." What I *really* meant, Alex thought, was were you by any chance on the sixth-floor observation deck of the tower when you noticed that your precious little memento was no longer fastened on your key chain?

The nasty thought shocked her. Marty? Marty would never hurt someone, not even someone he was really mad at. Certainly not

Kyle, one of his best buddies and fellow athletes.

But followed by the nasty thought came an equally nasty little voice from somewhere inside her head. Oh, come off it, the voice snarled, how do you know what Marty would or wouldn't do? You hardly know him, so quit pretending you've figured him out. He's cute, he has a good sense of humor, he dresses neatly, and he doesn't have bad breath. That's about the extent of your knowledge of this guy, so don't be so sure there isn't another side to him. There is to almost everybody, you know. So just don't be so sure.

Shut up, she ordered, and the voice subsided.

When they got to Vinnie's crowded parking lot, Alex felt some of the tension ooze out of her. Lots of people, lots and lots of people were inside that restaurant. That was good. Very good. With lots of people around her, she'd be safe. Unless . . . her heart leapfrogged . . . unless one of those people happened to be the one who had attacked Kyle.

And that person might know what *she* looked like, although she had no idea what *he* looked like.

Except, she recalled, there was something distinctive about him. If only she could figure out what it was, maybe she'd be able to pick him out of a crowd.

Inside, she sent the others to go search for that rarest of creatures on Sunday afternoon at Vinnie's — an empty booth — saying she had to go to the restroom.

But that's not where she went. Instead, when they'd left to make their way through the crowd standing around the jukebox, she turned and walked straight over to the red metal booth in the corner. She wanted to see The Wizard, wanted to check him out thoroughly. She had been planning to do this ever since she'd awakened that morning. The only way she was going to get rid of that horrible image of him from her nightmare was to face him and take a really good look at him.

When she was standing in front of him, uneasiness overtook her. This is the very spot, she thought, where Julie wished she didn't have the same "boring old face." And that same night, her face changed, probably forever. This is the very spot where Gabe wished for wheels, so he wouldn't have to walk so much. And that same night, his legs were injured so that he couldn't walk for a week. This is the very spot where Kyle complained about not having enough peace and quiet. And now Kyle is in a peaceful, quiet *coma*.

And so, she thought, if I didn't know better. . . .

She was afraid to look up, to confront the icy blue eyes. What if she saw something in them . . . ?

You're being ridiculous, she told herself. And lifted her head.

She stared straight at The Wizard. And noticed that the left ear, just below the edge of his tall pointed hat, was chipped. The paint on his right hand was peeling. His shirt was frayed at the cuffs.

She'd been afraid of *this*?

You are old, she telegraphed mentally to the pale, narrow face. You are old and falling apart, and perfectly harmless. Your days are numbered. I can't imagine now what I'm even doing here, why I had to see for myself that you couldn't possibly have had anything to do with the things that happened. I must have still been in shock. My brain wasn't working right.

And then she felt, suddenly, very sorry for the old toy. Its days really *were* numbered. Nobody wanted old, creaky, fraying fortunetellers now. Electronic gadgets, that was the thing: video games and computers and Nintendo, those were the present. This guy was obsolete.

Feeling sympathetic, Alex impulsively dug

into her pocket for a quarter. Why not? He wouldn't be getting many more. She could spare twenty-five cents.

"What are you doing over here all by yourself?"

Alex jumped, and dropped her quarter.

Marty bent to retrieve it. "I thought you didn't believe in this stuff."

"I don't. I was feeling sorry for the old guy. He's not getting much attention anymore."

"Nope. Too old-fashioned. Not exciting enough for our generation." He handed Alex the quarter. "What's a cynic like you doing throwing your hard-earned money away?"

She shrugged. "I thought it might be fun. Everyone else has done it." Yeah, and look what happened to *them*, the nasty little voice said. But now she could ignore it. "It's my turn."

Still, she hesitated when her hand reached the coin slot. The Wizard's glassy blue eyes stared at her, as if he were daring her to go for it. Go ahead, they seemed to say, but don't hold me responsible for what happens afterward.

"Scared?" Marty teased. "You don't have to do this, you know. You don't have to prove anything."

Stung, she dropped the coin into the slot.

The machine began to groan and creak and whirr.

"Maybe my card will say," she cracked as she reached down to pick it up, "that wealth and fame will be mine any minute now." She picked up the card and, taking a deep breath, read it silently. Disappointment filled her face.

"What?" Marty said, leaning over to peer down at the card in her hand.

"Oh, it's the same one you got. SILENCE IS GOLDEN. The machine is repeating itself. Vinnie better get some new cards if he wants people to keep putting quarters in." She tossed the card into a nearby trash can. "See? That just proves it doesn't mean anything, if people are getting the same cards."

Marty grinned. "I thought you were already convinced it didn't mean anything."

"I was. I *was!*"

It wasn't until they'd begun eating that Alex realized that while that particular card might not have held any meaning in Marty's case, it easily could in hers. *Silence is golden* . . . wasn't that, in effect, what the policeman had told her? That she needed to keep her lips zipped? If she hadn't known that Marty had already received an identical card, it might have shaken her up some. As if . . . as if The Wizard really did know what was going on in her life.

Chapter 12

There was so much gossip on campus about Kyle that Alex had to remind herself constantly over the next few days that silence, in her case, definitely was golden. She wanted so much to set the record straight, to announce to one and all that Kyle had not *jumped* from the tower, but she couldn't. She would have had to say how she knew that. If there was a chance that Kyle's attacker didn't know a witness existed, she wanted to keep it that way.

The police questioned her again, pressing for details. She mentioned that there was something odd about the second figure, but since she couldn't be any more specific than that, they let it drop.

When they'd gone, she concentrated on trying to remember what had seemed odd about the other person on the deck. His arm . . . something about his arm . . .

The following weekend there was an open house party at Delta Psi, the football fraternity. Alex didn't want to go.

But Jenny pleaded with her. "Come on, Alex, it'll be fun. Bennett and Marty are pledging there." Jenny smiled slyly. "And how *are* things with Marty?" she asked.

Alex shrugged. "He's been acting really weird lately. I guess he misses Kyle."

She went to the party, after all. Jenny was determined to go, and Alex was afraid to stay in the room alone. On a Friday night, the dorm would empty out fast. But there'd be plenty of people at the frat party. She'd be safe there.

Bennett was without crutches again, and insisted he'd be playing in the following day's game. "I've had enough therapy this week to cure twelve people," he said as he led Jenny out onto the dance floor. "And it's finally working."

Later, he asked Alex to dance, giving her the opportunity to ask him the same question she'd asked Marty. She asked Bennett if he'd received a golden football, like Marty and Kyle.

"Sure." He looked down at her. "Why?"

"Do you wear it?"

"No. I can't stand jewelry. Gets in the way. I brought it home to my folks' one weekend and left it there. Why?"

Alex saw Marty dancing with a tall blonde girl. He was laughing. "I just wondered. I think they're nice, but none of you seem to wear them. I mean, you're all so gung-ho over football, I'd think you'd love wearing something like that."

"Nah." Bennett shrugged. "I'm not into jewelry."

So it hadn't been Bennett's little football sitting in that plant. Not Bennett's, not Kyle's, and Marty had lost his.

Then whose was it?

Later, Alex talked with Gabe for a while. When she asked him about his football memento, he said, "Lost it a while ago. I can't keep track of stuff like that."

She hoped the guys wouldn't get together and compare notes. If they knew she'd asked each of them the same question about the little football, they'd think she was losing her grip.

Glancing around the room, she tried once again to remember exactly what had been so odd about Kyle's attacker. The arm . . . the arm had looked strange . . .

There wasn't a single abnormal-looking arm in the room.

By the time Marty finally asked her to dance, she was so annoyed with him, she barely spoke. She was relieved when the music ended.

Everyone else seemed to be having barrels of fun. Enough laughter to fill a funhouse, plenty of great music, good eats . . . but Alex wasn't having fun.

I'd rather be at the hospital talking to Julie, she thought, and jumped up. It wasn't that late. And if she took the shuttle, she'd be perfectly safe. Shuttle there, shuttle back . . . nothing risky about that.

She retrieved her coat, told Jenny that she was leaving, and hurried out of the house. She would wait for the shuttle right out in front. What could be safer than standing on a sidewalk in front of a house full of people?

It was cold outside, and smelled of rain to come. The wind was picking up and thick clouds hid the moon. Another storm on the way? Maybe she should forget about going into town and return to her room.

But she'd be alone there. Bad idea.

And Julie would be glad to see her. Maybe Kyle had improved. Kyle *had* to improve. He had to come out of his coma and identify his attacker. Then the police would arrest the guy and no one else would get hurt.

No one else, meaning *me*, Alex thought, and wished that she could tell someone how scared she was. It was hard, being scared all alone. But the small white card had read, SILENCE

IS GOLDEN, and in her case, the old Wizard was right on target. Talking about what she'd seen could get her in a whole lot of very nasty trouble.

She heard in the distance the telltale grinding gears of a shuttle bus. The relief that swept over her made her knees weak. In just a minute or two, she'd be safe on the bus with other people around her, and she'd certainly be safe at the hospital.

A minute later, the yellow bus pulled up under the streetlight, and Alex climbed aboard. The shuttle was free. No stopping to deposit a coin. Her eyes swept the seats ahead of her.

They were all empty.

There was no one else on the bus. That was odd. Then again, it was the middle of a Friday evening. People who had plans had probably already gone where they were going.

Alex found a seat in the middle and flopped into it. Getting away from campus for a little while would be good. She needed the break.

She settled back in her seat, gazing out the window. When they pulled onto the highway toward Twin Falls, houses began flying by and she played a game she'd played on long road trips when she was a child . . . who lived in the houses, what were they doing, did they have children, a dog? a cat? The houses continued to fly by . . .

In fact . . . Alex sat up straighter . . . they were flying by too fast. Much too fast.

"Hey!" she called up to the driver, "where's the fire? I'm not in any big rush. And I'd like to get there in one piece."

The shuttle failed to slow down, even a little. Instead, it seemed to Alex that it picked up even more speed.

They were going much, much too fast.

"Driver!" she yelled over the sound of the motor, "would you please slow *down?*"

Faster, faster . . . the small yellow bus began switching lanes rapidly, weaving in and out of traffic, its tires squealing. Horns honked, drivers yelled out their windows, but the bus never slowed.

Alex fought to still a rising sense of panic.

The back of the driver's seat was high, hiding him from Alex's view. Her eyes went to the rearview mirror. Ordinarily, you could see the driver's face reflected in the mirror from where she was sitting. She'd noticed that before. But not now. The mirror had been tilted, at an angle, reflecting nothing but the aisle between the seats.

The bus continued to careen down the highway.

Praying for a traffic cop, Alex cried, "I'm going to have to report you for this! And I will. I *will* do that, if you don't stop this bus and let me off! *Now!*"

When there was no response, she stood up, clutching the edge of the seat in front of her for support. She would go to the front of the bus and confront the crazy driver directly, make him stop.

Suddenly, the bus veered wildly, knocking her off balance. She toppled to her knees in the aisle as the bus careened across two lanes of traffic and dove off the highway and onto a dirt road splitting an area of deep woods. At no time did the bus reduce its speed.

Alex struggled to her feet, clutching the seat beside her. "What are you *doing*?" she screamed, "*what?*" There was nothing but thick, dark woods on both sides of them now, no friendly houses, no other cars . . . nothing but blackness and the shadowy outlines of bare tree branches reaching to the sky. "Let me *out of here!* Stop this bus right *now!*"

It didn't stop. It didn't even slow down, in spite of the beating it was taking from hurtling over the holes and bumps and ridges of a seldom-traveled dirt road.

She still couldn't see the driver. But she could see, as she swayed back and forth clutching the edge of a seat, what looked like the hem of an old tan raincoat. It was dragging on the floor beside the driver's seat.

There shouldn't be an old tan raincoat there, she thought, struggling to stay afoot. The shuttle bus drivers wear navy-blue uniforms, and they're not dirty or worn.

Still holding on for dear life, she leaned backward in the aisle as far as she could, craning her neck to catch a glimpse of the driver behind that high seat. All she could see was a huge, dirty gray hat, yanked down to meet the top of the raincoat, as if he didn't want anyone to see him.

And she knew then, that it was *him.*

He *had* seen her standing in Amber's window the night he tried to kill Kyle.

He knew who she was.

And he had come for her.

Chapter 13

The yellow bus continued to race over the dirt road through the woods, twisting, turning, never slowing down, its headlights splitting the darkness before it.

Gripping the edge of a seat so hard her knuckles turned white and her arms began to ache fiercely, Alex's eyes searched frantically for a way out. Some of the shuttles had back doors . . . wide ones, for wheelchair access. If this was one of those buses, she could kick those doors open. . . .

There was no back door.

She was trapped on a racing bus with a maniac. A maniac who wanted her dead, and apparently didn't care if he died, too.

"What are you going to *do*?" she screamed. "Are you going to kill us both?" Was that what he had in mind? Because if the bus crashed at this speed, he would certainly die, too.

But *I* don't want to die, Alex thought clearly.

And then, in the next moment, she heard the siren. At first she thought she was imagining it, wishing it. But her head whipped around and there it was, a big, beautiful, wonderful police car, its round blue light whirling on the roof.

She almost cried from sheer joy. She wasn't going to *die*! The police were here. They would save her. That was their job. They wouldn't let a perfectly innocent person die at the hands of a maniac.

Alex had no idea what to do. Staying put seemed the best idea, until the policemen caught up with them.

She hung on.

The bus whipped around a sharp curve, and she fell, slamming her head against the side of a seat. Dizziness overwhelmed her, her hands released their grip, and she sank to the floor, landing on her back. Without something to hold onto, she was tossed back and forth, her back and shoulders slamming repeatedly into the base of one seat or another. It hurt, and she cried out in pain.

Had to get up . . . had to . . . she was helpless like this . . .

Gritting her teeth, she reached up and fastened one hand around the curved metal handle of a seat back, and began slowly pulling herself upward again.

When she was in a sitting position, her eyes went to the front of the bus. There was movement there. She watched, disbelieving, as the dirty tan raincoat threw itself off the seat and rolled itself up into a ball, the floppy old rain hat covering any features.

Alex stared, wide-eyed.

The ball of raincoat tumbled, end over end, down the steps.

And as it tumbled, Alex heard the evil sound from her nightmare: the low, wicked *hahaha-haha*. . . .

The doors opened.

The bundle of raincoat dove through the opening.

The doors closed.

Alex heard the sinister laughter for several moments after the doors closed.

Frozen in shock, it took her several minutes to understand what had happened. When she did, she nearly fainted with terror.

There was no one at the wheel!

Chapter 14

Everything became a blur after that.

Alex had never learned to drive.

Crying and shaking, she managed to pull herself to her feet and make her way up the aisle. When she slid into the driver's seat, she did it in a state of shock and had no memory of it afterward. Later, the policemen told her that she did a great job of steering the bus, keeping it from careening off the road, until, no longer being fed gas, it finally slowed and, gradually, bumped to a stop against an embankment.

But she remembered none of that. The last thing she remembered was that evil, blood-chilling *hahahahahah* as the raincoat went out the door of the bus. The sound still rang in her ears.

They told her they had a hard time getting her fingers to uncurl from around the steering wheel. She didn't remember ever touching the steering wheel.

When she was sitting safely in the police car, she asked tremulously, "Did you catch him? He went into the woods, I think."

"No, miss," the driver said. "I let my partner here out of the car when we saw the guy jump, and he followed on foot for some distance, but the guy must have been moving pretty fast. No sign of him. Disappeared into thin air, seems like."

"I can't believe he wasn't killed when he jumped," Alex said. "The bus was going so fast. How could anyone survive that?"

"Don't know, Miss. But he did. And in good health, I'd guess, or he wouldn't have eluded Ryan here. Could be hiding somewhere around here. We'll take you home and then organize a search. We'll find him, don't you worry."

Right. What on earth did she have to worry about? She was safe in a police car, wasn't she? If only she could stay there forever. "How did you know we were out here, in the middle of nowhere?" she asked.

"Some concerned citizen with a car phone called in and said there was a maniac on the highway doing figure eights with a university shuttle bus. He saw you take that detour onto Old Sawmill Road. You sure you're okay?"

To Alex's complete astonishment, she really was okay. No blood, nothing broken, and most important of all, *alive*. She was alive.

The other surprising thing was that it took the policemen only a few minutes to drive her back to her dorm.

"We were this close to school?" she asked incredulously. "Right around the corner from it?"

The policeman opening the door for her nodded. "Yep. Your driver made a couple of U-turns. You were actually just behind one of the off-campus dorms — Nightingale Hall."

Alex shuddered. It figured that was where her own nightmare had taken place.

They sat in the empty lobby at Lester, where the policemen asked her endless questions. Alex had never felt so stupid. She had been warned against going anywhere alone. Not only had she left the party alone, she'd climbed aboard a bus empty of other passengers. But it had never occurred to her to be wary of a bus driver.

The officers stood up. "If we don't find the guy when we search the woods, we'll talk to the captain about putting a guard on you," one of them said.

But when they'd walked her to her room and left, Alex cringed at the idea of some police officer following her around all over campus all day long. People would stare at her. She would hate that.

They'd probably catch the guy. He must have hurt *something* when he dove off that speeding bus. He was probably holed up in the woods somewhere, nursing his wounds, and they'd catch him before he could get away.

Then she'd be safe again.

She locked the door before crawling underneath the covers to wait, wide awake, for Jenny to come home. Periodically, she would begin shaking violently and would have to bite down on her lower lip, hard, to calm down.

Jenny came home in a bad mood.

"They all went off somewhere without me!" she cried, tossing her purse on the bed. "Marty, Bennett, Gabe . . . I couldn't believe it! I had to walk back with Jill and Amber."

Alex, who would cheerfully have settled for a nice, safe walk home instead of an insane bus ride, sat up. "Where did they go? The guys, I mean?"

Jenny flopped down on her bed and leaned against the wall. "Gabe said his legs were bothering him and he wanted to call Julie, so he left. And then Marty found out you were gone, so he left, too."

Alex didn't see why. It wasn't as if he'd been

clinging to her like a vine at the party.

"And then Bennett left. Said he needed his rest for the 'big game' tomorrow. I got mad. I mean, we'd been having so much fun, I didn't want him to leave. A little while later, I was sorry I'd lost my temper, and called him to apologize. He wasn't there."

"Maybe he was asleep. Like he said, big game tomorrow."

Jenny shook her head. "I'll bet anything he went down to Vinnie's. He's been spending so much time there lately. He's obsessed with that stupid fortune-teller."

Alex felt a chill. "The Wizard?"

"Yeah. Everyone else is pretty bored with it by now, but not Bennett. And," Jenny pulled her hair loose from its ponytail and let it fall around her shoulders, "I saw Marty and Gabe hanging around it a couple of times this week, too." She shrugged. "I don't get what they see in it myself. I thought it would be fun, too, at first. But the cards are so stupid. They don't mean a thing."

True . . . unless you witness an attempted murder and The Wizard gives you a card that says SILENCE IS GOLDEN, Alex thought. *That* could certainly mean something.

But then, Alex reminded herself, Marty had received the same card. Jenny was right. The cards didn't mean anything. It wasn't as if she'd received a card that said BEWARE OF YELLOW BUSES. *That* would have meant something.

"How was Julie?" Jenny asked suddenly.

And Alex remembered that she had been on her way to the hospital when she'd been . . . hijacked. Could she tell Jenny what had happened? She wanted to tell *someone*. Maybe saying it out loud would make it seem, somehow, not so terrible.

But telling Jenny might be putting her in danger, too. If the police didn't catch the guy tonight or tomorrow . . . horrible thought . . . he would still be on the loose. And he might guess that she had told her roommate. No, Jenny mustn't know. For her own sake.

"I never got there. I decided I was too tired, so I just came home." The lie came more easily than she'd thought it would. Maybe because it was for a good reason.

As she rolled over and tried to go to sleep, a sound echoed in her head . . . a deep, evil *hahahahahaha*.

Chapter 15

Alex awoke in the morning exhausted.

She had to fight the urge to stay in bed, under the covers all day. But she refused to hide in her room for the rest of her life. Besides, it was beautiful outside, clear and crisp, with a bright blue, cloudless sky. Another perfect football day. At the stadium, surrounded by classmates and friends, Alex tried to shed the terror of her crazy bus ride. If only the phone had rung before she and Jenny left their room, if only the police had called with good news. . . .

Was he still out there somewhere?

Not only did Marty receive a few minutes of playing time in the game, but to Alex's surprise, so did Gabe and Bennett. Bennett was brilliant, throwing a tricky pass that earned a last-minute touchdown.

"I can't believe Coach let Gabe play," Alex

told Jenny as they waited outside the stadium for the boys. They were all going to Vinnie's for pizza.

"Why not? He let Bennett play, and Bennett's been on crutches, too. Gabe got his stitches out Wednesday, Julie told me. And he probably wore lots of padding today. Anyway, it was only for a few minutes, Alex. I heard Coach telling Prof Pagnozi that we're going to have a super team next year. Championship caliber, he said." Her expression grew dreamy. "And I know he meant because of Bennett. Wasn't he great today?" She sighed. "I've never gone out with a football star before. Julie dated all the star athletes in high school. But not me. I always wanted to."

Gabe and Bennett both insisted they were fine, when Alex asked. And she noticed that neither one of them was limping. Playing for those few minutes didn't seem to have done any further damage.

At Vinnie's, Alex was relieved to find that no one had heard any rumors about a wild bus ride on a dirt road behind the school. If they had, they would have been gossiping about it. They might have asked questions. And she wouldn't have had any answers.

But she was disappointed, when she called the police station from Vinnie's pay phone, to learn that the hijacker hadn't been caught, yet.

She couldn't believe it. How far could he have gone? He *must* have hurt himself when he dove off that bus. How could he *not* have?

Crestfallen, she replaced the receiver on the wall phone. When she turned around, she was staring straight into the eyes of The Wizard.

"You're supposed to know so much," she demanded, "why don't *you* tell me what's going on?"

And then, before she could move away, the arm clanked and whirred and lifted, and when she looked, there was a card in the little cup on the outside of the booth.

"But I didn't put a quarter in," she protested even as curiosity moved her to reach out and take the card. "Business is so bad, you're giving them away free now?"

Marty suddenly appeared around the corner. His face was badly bruised from an encounter with the opposing team's tackle, and he was walking very stiffly. "You here again?" he teased, apparently forgetting that he'd been annoyed with her for leaving the party the night before. "Can't stay away from this guy, can you? Should I be jealous?"

"I thought it was *you* who couldn't stay away," she said coolly. "You and Bennett and Gabe. Jenny said you guys hang around this thing a lot. I wanted to see if I was missing something about Old Stoneface here, so I decided to give him a shot." She didn't tell Marty that she hadn't deposited a coin.

"So, what's the card say?" he asked.

Alex looked down at the card. And her mouth fell open. "I . . . I . . ." She had been prepared to shrug and say the card didn't mean anything. That was what she had planned to do. Expected to do.

But she couldn't.

Because what the card said was, THE WHEELS ON THE BUS GO ROUND AND ROUND.

"Hey, I know that song!" Marty said when he'd read the card. "We used to sing it on the way to summer camp." He began singing. "The wheels on the bus go round and round, round and round, round and round . . ."

"Shut up!" Alex snapped.

"What? What's wrong? You look sick. It's just a kids' song, right?"

Alex looked up, directly into the eyes of The Wizard. Wasn't he . . . smiling? Weren't his red-painted lips curved up, just a little?

She was losing her mind. Who could blame her, after the week she'd had?

"It is kind of weird, though," Marty said. "I

mean, a kids' song? That's not anything like all the other cards we got."

She didn't want to talk about it. She couldn't. "C'mon, I'm starving," she urged, tugging at Marty's hand. She had to get away from those cruel blue eyes.

She could swear, as she turned away, that The Wizard's lips had curved upward another inch.

"Alex?" Marty turned her toward him and looked down into her face. "What's going on? You've been acting really off the wall lately."

"Look who's talking," she retorted. "You haven't exactly been Mr. Congeniality."

"You're right. It's that speech. For soc. Just can't get it right. I know what I want to say, but I can't put the words together right. You helped a lot with the early draft, but now I'm stuck on the last part, and it's due Monday. I'll be working on it all weekend."

Any other time, she might have been sympathetic. But she couldn't worry about Marty's speech now. Besides, he'd ace it. He liked talking, especially in front of a crowd. He'd be fine.

"Good luck," was all she said as she led him to the booth commandeered by Gabe and Bennett.

When Kiki arrived a few minutes later, Alex almost didn't recognize her. She was wearing a bright orange blouse, tucked into her jeans, and the jeans hung on her hips. Her cheekbones jutted out sharply. But instead of looking beautiful, as Alex had anticipated, Kiki looked tired and haggard. There were dark circles around her eyes and a sullen look about her.

They found out why immediately. "I've been suspended from the soccer team," she told them angrily. "Coach says I'm way under my weight." Her upper lip curled disdainfully. "She says she's afraid I'll get hurt. Can you believe it? I've been playing soccer since I was ten and I've never had so much as a bruised knee cap. The woman is crazy!"

She slid into the booth. Alex couldn't help noticing how little room she needed now.

"Well," Bennett said calmly, "you *are* thinner. Maybe your coach is right. How come you lost so much? Thought you were just going to shed a few pounds."

A look of bewilderment came over Kiki's face. "Well, I meant to," she said. "I guess it just felt so good to take off the excess, I got carried away. But I'm eating now."

She ate more pizza than anyone else at the table.

When Kiki had first approached the table, Alex's instinctive reaction had been, She's sick. Kiki's sick, and she doesn't even know it. But now, watching her eat, she wondered if that could possibly be true. What kind of illness left a person with that kind of appetite? When *she* was sick, the last thing she felt like doing was eating.

"Too bad about soccer," Marty told Kiki sympathetically. "I know what it feels like not to play a sport you love. It's the worst. You'd do almost anything to get back in the game."

Bennett and Gabe nodded vigorously.

Kiki nodded, too. But she didn't stop eating.

Alex tried to eat something, too. She hadn't been eating enough lately. She didn't want to end up looking like Kiki.

She couldn't stop thinking about the fortune-telling card. THE WHEELS ON THE BUS GO ROUND AND ROUND . . . The song began skittering around inside her head and refused to leave.

No one but the police knew about that terrifying bus ride. No one . . .

Well . . . there *was* one other person who knew.

She hadn't paid for that card. She hadn't deposited a coin. Someone could have put that card in the little cup earlier, before she got there. But . . . how would he have known that she was going to make a phone call? How could he have known that she'd be back there, by The Wizard?

Unless . . . her heart began to pound loudly in her chest . . . unless he was *there*! Watching her. . . .

Alex shrank back against the seat. I really am crazy, she thought, breaking out in an icy sweat. Here I am, going to football games and eating at Vinnie's, as if everything is normal, when I know . . . I *know* someone wants me dead. What's wrong with me? I should be hiding in my room with the door locked, or hiring a bodyguard, or asking the police for protection.

"Alex," Jenny was saying, "what's the matter?"

"I have to go," Alex said abruptly. "Marty, will you please take me home?"

"What's wrong?" Kiki asked, wiping her mouth. "Are you sick? You look terrible."

Look who's talking, Alex thought but didn't say. "Headache. Marty?" She could tell by the expression on his face that he wasn't keen on leaving.

"If you don't want to," she told Marty, "I can take the shuttle." But she knew she couldn't. Could she ever take it again? Maybe, a thousand years from now. But not tonight.

"No, that's okay. I'll take you." Marty slid out of the booth.

But when they got outside, Alex changed her mind about going back to campus. It was Saturday. No one would be in the dorm. It wasn't a good idea to go back to an empty room in an empty dorm.

Alex felt the sting of tears pressing against her eyelids. This wasn't fair at all. She hadn't done anything wrong. Why did she have to be afraid?

Immediately ashamed, remembering how much worse things were for Julie and Kyle, she knew suddenly where she wanted to go.

"Will you take me to the hospital?" she asked when they were in the car.

"I thought you wanted to go home. What about your headache?"

"Marty, could you practice being a human being tonight? Just for this one night? I haven't seen Julie enough lately, and I'd also like to find out how *your* best friend is, if you don't mind."

"Sorry," he muttered, and started the car.

She hadn't meant to be so snotty. After all, Marty had no idea what was going on. Maybe she should tell him about seeing Kyle thrown off that deck. Marty had a right to know that his best friend hadn't tried to commit suicide.

But then, he already knew that. She'd heard him say it a dozen times. "Not Leavitt, not in a million years, he wouldn't jump off a tower." He was already positive about that. No need to tell him.

And if she told him about the murderous bus ride, he'd freak. Would he even believe her? He'd already said she'd been acting weird.

Alex knew that she probably would have told him if they'd been getting along better. But lately he seemed so uptight, so annoyed. Besides, if he'd paid more attention to her at the frat party, she probably never would have left, never would have hopped the shuttle. . . .

She didn't say another word until they got to the hospital. He didn't, either.

But when they left the car and headed for the hospital entrance, he took her hand and said, "Alex, you're right. Sorry I've been such a jerk lately. It'll pass, I promise. As soon as I get that speech over with."

"Right. Forget it. Sorry I bit your head off."

While Marty went to check out Kyle's condition, Alex visited Julie.

Julie was hurt that Jenny hadn't been around much. "I know my folks are here now, and that's nice," she said. "But Jenny tells me stuff about school, and my parents can't do that. And they're so worried about what my face is going to look like, it gets real tense in here some-times."

"I think she's in love," Alex said. "With Bennett."

Julie nodded. "I know. When she calls me, that's all she talks about." Her voice softened. "It's like she's having all the fun she missed in high school. I had it, but Jenny never did. It's kind of weird that I had to get hurt for Jenny to have fun, don't you think?"

Alex hadn't thought of it that way. But then she remembered Jenny twirling in front of the mirror in Julie's clothes, her hair curled, makeup on . . . To hide the odd sensation that image suddenly created, she said hastily, "I'm sure Jenny would take away the accident if she could."

But, remembering the look on Jenny's face when Bennett threw that pass, Alex wondered *how* sure she was about that.

Julie brightened then, and said, "Gabe was in this morning, before the game. And he said he'd like me to wear his gold football. You know, those little ones the guys got when they made the team?" Julie smiled, and for just a second, in spite of the roadmap of tape on her face and the stitches and bruises, Alex saw the old Julie. "It's kind of like being engaged to be engaged to be engaged, right? It comes on a chain. I'll wear it around my neck."

Even as Alex hugged Julie, she was thinking, But Gabe told me he'd *lost* his football. He must have found it. That was fast.

Maybe mentioning it to him at the dance had given him the idea to hunt for it and give it to Julie.

She was still thinking about Gabe's gold football when she arrived at the intensive care unit to meet Marty. And she thought about it when she looked through the glass window and saw Kyle still lying there, motionless. Marty had gone to grab a Coke from the machine before leaving the hospital, and when Alex's eyes caught sight of the familiar brown envelope lying on the counter behind the nurse's station, she looked around to see if anyone was watching.

She loved Gabe Russo. Everyone loved Gabe Russo. But that little gold football she'd found in the plant on the deck was the only clue she had to who had pushed Kyle over that wall. Gabe had told her he'd lost his football. Now, suddenly, he'd found it? He'd been right here in the hospital for quite a while, and still came in for therapy. Gabe would have known that Kyle wore his football around his neck, and that it would be in the envelope with the rest of his belongings. All he had to do was open it, as she had, and reach inside . . .

Gabe? No, not possible . . .

But if he had Kyle's football, no one could accuse him of having lost his own up on the tower.

Hardly able to bear what she was thinking, Alex knew she had no choice. She had seen for herself that Kyle's football was safely inside that envelope. If it was still there, she would hate herself later for doubting Gabe.

She darted around the corner, yanked open the envelope flap for the second time, and thrust her hand inside.

And although her fingers searched and probed as long as she dared, and although they met the soft leather of a wallet and the hard metal of jangling keys and the round smoothness of coins, they never touched anything even faintly resembling the oval shape of a tiny gold football.

It was gone.

Chapter 16

Alex was just about to replace the envelope when a voice cried from behind her, "Just exactly what do you think you're doing?"

Cringing guiltily, Alex yanked her hand free and dropped the envelope. And whirled to face an angry nurse.

"I . . . I just . . ." Thinking quickly, Alex took a deep breath and said, "Kyle Leavitt is my boyfriend. I was wearing his little gold football and then we had a fight and I gave it back to him, but now that he's sick, I want it back. I thought it would be in here, with his things. But it isn't."

The nurse regarded her with suspicion. "Listen, I don't know what you're up to, Miss, but you're wrong about the football. It *is* in there. Put it in there myself, the night he was brought in."

"It's not there now."

"Let me see." The nurse dumped the envelope's contents onto the desk. There was no tiny gold ornament. Frowning, she looked up at Alex. "You sure you didn't already take it out of here?"

"No. If I had, I'd be wearing it around my neck."

"Well, I don't know then. Like I said, it was here. Should have locked this envelope in the cupboard in back, but I never got around to it. I'll do it now." And the envelope was whisked away.

Alex spent the rest of the weekend wondering what had happened to Kyle's charm. She had felt it, inside that envelope, with her own fingers. It had *been* there. Now, it wasn't. Why would someone take it?

The answer came several times: to replace one that was missing. Each time, she rejected that answer. Because Marty had lost *his*. So had Gabe. And Bennett didn't seem to know where his was, either. If any one of them had lost their own golden football up on that sixth-floor observation deck, they wouldn't want anyone to know it. So they would want it replaced, wouldn't they? And they would know that Kyle had been wearing his when he went over that wall, and where to look for it. Gabe had been right here in the hospital. So had Marty. And Bennett came here for his therapy.

But every single one of them was a good friend of Kyle's. Why would they have done something so terrible to him?

They wouldn't have.

Reminding herself that there were other guys who owned those football charms, Alex pushed the nasty thoughts out of her mind, and called the police to see if they'd made any progress.

They hadn't. No fingerprints on the bus, no trace of anyone in the woods . . . no luck at all.

They wanted, she was told, to put a guard on her, but they couldn't spare the manpower right now, in the middle of a big investigation like this. The police department in the town of Twin Falls was not a large one. "Best that you not go out alone," the desk sergeant told her sternly, and she promised that she wouldn't.

He promised to let her know the minute something solid "came up."

At lunch in the dining hall on Sunday, Alex was sitting with Jill and Amber when Kiki walked in. The change in her was shocking. Her hair hung lank and oily around her ears, her face was pale and wan, her eyes shadowed. And her clothes hung on her.

"What *is* it with that girl?" Jill said, watching

as Kiki loaded a tray with food. "She eats like a horse, but she looks like a twig. I don't get it. If I ate like that, I'd look like the Goodyear blimp."

"I think there's something wrong with her," Alex said, her eyes on Kiki as she moved lethargically toward a seat in the corner and sat down. "I think she's sick. She really should see a doctor."

The words were barely out of her mouth when Kiki's eyes rolled back in her head and she slid out of her chair onto the floor, landing in a soft, limp heap.

When she had been taken to the infirmary, Alex said quietly, "Well, at least she'll get help. They'll find out what's wrong with her now."

It wasn't until later that night as she was teetering on the edge of sleep that she remembered Kiki's wish at Vinnie's the first night they'd seen The Wizard, the night of that wild lightning strike. Kiki had wished she would lose weight, just as Julie had wished for a different face and Gabe had wished he didn't have to walk so much.

Alex turned restlessly in her bed. If it wasn't the most idiotic thing in the world to think, she would think The Wizard had been listening when they spoke that night. *Wishes Granted.* . . . said the sign on the front of the red booth. And what had her grandmother always told her? "Be careful what you wish for, Alexandria. You just might *get* it!"

In a perverse, twisted way, Julie, Gabe, and Kyle had all got what they'd asked for. Not in the way they'd wanted it, of course. Maybe her grandmother had been right.

Crazy way to think . . . The Wizard had no power to grant wishes. He was just a mechanical figure, an old, fraying one at that.

The only thing I wished for, she thought uneasily, was to forget about The Wizard.

Then Alex heard in her head, the song, *The wheels on the bus go round and round, round and round, round and round, the wheels on the bus go round and round, all through the town.*

No one but she and her hijacker had known about the terrifying bus ride. So how did that card get into the fortune-telling booth? Unless . . . unless . . .

No! Crazy, crazy. . . . Be careful, Alex, she warned, rolling over and thrusting her face into her pillow, or you'll be the next one carted off to the hospital. The *mental* hospital.

She fell asleep and dreamed she had been fastened into a white straitjacket, her arms tied behind her.

When she awoke, both arms were hopelessly tangled in the sheets.

She tried to laugh, and found it impossible.

She didn't want to go to class. The idea of staying in her room with the door locked made more sense than ever. And she could afford to miss a few classes.

But Marty was giving his speech today in sociology. She couldn't miss that.

She quickly showered, and dressed in jeans and her favorite bright red blouse. Then she woke Jenny, who had come in late again, and waited while Jenny dressed. She grumbled crankily the entire time, but she didn't want to miss Marty's speech, either.

Grateful that they'd already delivered their own speeches, the two girls hurried across campus to the mixed media lecture hall in the communications building.

The big, square room was packed when they arrived. Bennett and Gabe were already seated on the far side of the room, Bennett's legs propped up on an old radiator. He was enjoying hearty slaps on the back and shouted "congratulations" for his success in the game on Saturday. "He's positively glowing with triumph," Alex murmured to Jenny. "He certainly loves attention." Alex quickly realized that Jenny, too, was "glowing."

"I *know* what it's like to go without that," she told Alex, and sat down behind Bennett. Alex sat across the aisle, in front of Gabe.

Marty, in a blue V-necked sweater and jeans, was positioned behind the podium at the front of the hall. Although he didn't seem at all nervous, Alex flashed him an encouraging smile.

Dr. Taylor-Guinn, a tall, thin woman with thick black hair, had seated herself in front of the massive oak desk behind the podium, her hands folded in her lap, an expectant look on her face.

That's because, Alex thought, she knows Marty's speech will be one of the better ones. Everyone in the room who knows Marty knows it'll be a good speech. There was an air of relief in the room, a sense that while many of the recent speeches had been dry and painfully boring, there just might be a few good laughs in this one.

Marty waited patiently until all of the coughs, the clearing of throats, rattling of papers, and shuffling of feet had ended. Then he stood up very straight, shoulders back, head up, eyes focused on his audience in the stance that Dr. Taylor-Guinn had advised.

Watching him, Alex wished that she and Marty could get beyond whatever was between them lately. True, they'd all been on edge, and with good reason. But she and Marty were snapping each other's heads off half the time, and she didn't know why. She didn't think *he* did, either.

A respectful silence finally descended upon the room.

Marty cleared his throat one last time, glanced down at his notes, lifted his head, looked at his audience, and opened his mouth.

No sound emerged.

Surprise widened Marty's eyes. He had expected a sentence to come forth, and it hadn't.

He tried again, forming his lips to create words.

But the words were stillborn.

Alex had helped him with the research on his speech. She knew what he was trying to say. The title of his speech was *Coming of Age with the Computer.* It was a lighthearted look at how technology had changed society. And Alex knew the first line by heart: *The most significant difference between man, that creature known as* homo sapiens, *and the computer is, if you can't stand the way the computer is behaving, you can always unplug it. Don't you wish we could sometimes do that with people?*

But in that entire room, only Alex and Marty

knew what he was trying to say. Because he couldn't *say* it.

He tried. He tried again and again. His cheekbones flushed scarlet, the cords in his neck strained, and his eyes grew more and more bewildered as his mouth moved desperately to push forth words that refused to come.

Behind him, the communications professor shifted impatiently in her seat, and cleared her throat.

She can't see his face, Alex thought, sitting up very straight in her chair, wanting passionately to help in some way. Dr. Taylor-Guinn thinks Marty's stalling, that he's unprepared. Or maybe she thinks he's got stage fright. But he doesn't. I know he doesn't. Not Marty.

She saw Gabe and Bennett exchange embarrassed glances, and she wanted to slap them. *They* were embarrassed? It was *Marty* who was up there in front of the entire class, not them.

She watched in agony as Marty tried several more times, his face deepening in color, his fists clenching and unclenching with the effort. Twice, his eyes sought Alex's, as if to beg for help.

For one long moment, she thought about going up to the podium and giving the speech for him. She could do it. She knew enough about the material, and his notes would be well-organized.

But the teacher would never allow it. And, more important, Marty would be even more humiliated if she took over for him.

She stayed put. There was nothing she could do.

He had lost his voice.

People began coughing, clearing their throats, shuffling their feet in embarrassment for him. Alex was grateful that no one snickered.

When, finally giving up, Marty turned in misery to his professor, she took pity on him and coolly dismissed him.

Although he kept his head high and his back straight as he left the podium, Alex could feel his burning humiliation.

"Well," Jenny whispered sympathetically as another student replaced Marty at the front of the room, "Marty wished he could get out of giving his speech, remember? At Vinnie's, the night of the storm."

And Alex *did* remember then. She turned her head to look at him. He was sitting off to her left, looking totally bewildered. One hand repeatedly rubbed his throat.

He had made that wish, that night at Vinnie's, just as Julie, Gabe, and Kiki had made wishes.

And now Marty, like the others, had got what he wanted. He hadn't had to give the speech, after all. Hadn't been *able* to.

Then Alex remembered the fortune Marty had received from The Wizard, the same one she'd received.

She could see the small, crisp white card as it lay in Marty's hand that night of the storm. The print jumped up to meet her eyes.

SILENCE IS GOLDEN.

Chapter 17

Alex was waiting in the infirmary waiting room for Marty when Shelley, the tall redhead Bennett had once dated, walked in. She was wearing her drum majorette's outfit, and she was limping. "That stupid trombone player stepped on my foot," she complained as she hopped over to the counter. "And I have to march Saturday! Of all the luck . . ."

Alex sat patiently while Shelley checked in and was told to wait. When she was seated opposite Alex, the temptation to ask a few questions was too strong to ignore. Nonchalantly thumbing through a magazine, Alex said, "Didn't you used to date Bennett Stark?"

"Who are you?" Shelley asked rudely, rubbing her injured ankle.

"Alex Edgar. I'm a friend of Bennett's."

"Bennett . . . Bennett . . . oh, the rookie football player. Ex-football player, I should say. Yeah, I went out with him for a while. Why?" Her eyes narrowed. "He hasn't been talking about me, has he?"

"No, of course not. I just wondered . . . Bennett's been dating my roommate, and he wants to give her that little gold football of his," Alex lied. "You know, the one all the freshmen players received? But he can't find it. I just wondered if he might have given it to you and then forgotten about it."

She expected Shelley to say she didn't have it, that she'd never received it, that he really had taken it home and left it there.

But Shelley didn't say that. "Yeah, he gave it to me," she said instead. "It was cute. Not real gold, of course, but it didn't look half-bad with my blue cashmere."

Alex turned a page of her magazine. "Do you still have it?" Bennett *could* have forgotten that he'd given it to Shelley.

"It wasn't *that* cute. I gave it back to Bennett, natch. I knew if I kept it, he'd think there was still hope, and there wasn't."

Bennett's little gold football, identical to the one she'd found in the plant on the deck, wasn't back home as Bennett had said. It never had been. Not too awfully long ago, he'd given it to Shelley. And she'd given it back.

He couldn't have forgotten that.

Why had he lied?

Gabe, too, had lied . . . maybe. He was going to give *his* football to Julie, after telling Alex that he didn't know where it was.

Neither one of those things means anything, Alex told herself sternly. Gabe could have simply found his, and maybe Bennett hadn't wanted to tell her the embarrassing truth — that Shelley had handed his back.

She couldn't believe either one of them would have hurt Kyle. They were all *friends!*

But . . . then she remembered, that boy in the stands had said at the game, "Gabe wouldn't have played if Kyle was here."

Oh, for pete's sake, football couldn't be a motive for what had happened to Kyle. That was totally ridiculous!

Wasn't it?

Shelley was called in to be treated. Marty still hadn't come back out, so Alex decided she'd ask about Kiki. She hadn't seen her on campus. If she was still here, in the infirmary, she must be pretty sick.

"Yes, she's here," the nurse behind the reception desk told Alex. She clucked her tongue. "You kids and your crazy fad diets! That girl is *very* ill. We're transferring her to the hospital today." The middle-aged woman looked at

Alex with disapproving eyes. "She *was* on a diet, am I right?"

Alex nodded. "But she *was* eating. I saw her eat."

No reply.

"Could I see her, please?"

"I don't see why not. She hasn't had many visitors. Can't help feeling sorry for her. But we don't know how to treat eating disorders here. That girl is anorexic, you mark my words."

Alex's jaw dropped. Kiki? An eating disorder? She pictured Kiki helping herself to Julie's cookies and candy. "It isn't anything like that," she protested.

The nurse arched a graying eyebrow. "They're very good at hiding it, you know. Even their families seldom know until the problem is out of control. Go ahead in. Room four."

Alex walked down the hall and entered the small white room. But the patient lying in the bed there bore no resemblance to healthy, stocky, ruddy-cheeked Kiki Duff, pride of Salem's women's soccer team.

The girl in the bed seemed shrunken. She was frail and gaunt. Her head turned listlessly from side to side on the white pillow. The face was without color except for purplish shadows under sunken eyes. The cheekbones were hollow, the hair dull and sparse. Above the neck-line of a white hospital gown, a sharply etched collarbone jutted skyward.

Alex stood at the foot of the bed, paralyzed with horror. That couldn't be Kiki in the bed. It was a mistake . . . had to be . . .

But when she reached out and picked up the chart hanging on the bed rail, there was Kiki's name, plain as day: DUFF, KIKI.

No . . . no.

Alex leaned against the bed rail, and heard Kiki's voice in her head, saying, "I'm going to wish I were five pounds thinner." She hadn't made the wish that night. No one had had a quarter. But had she gone back later and made that same wish?

And . . . had it been *granted?*

I have to stop pretending all of this is just coincidence, Alex thought, her hands shaking as she replaced Kiki's chart. It *can't* be. Not *all* of it.

She walked over to stand beside Kiki's bed. Kiki wouldn't deliberately starve herself. Whatever was wrong with her, it was beyond her control.

Impulsively, Alex reached down to gently stroke the skeletal cheek.

The sunken eyes opened. Tears slid weakly down the gaunt cheekbones. The mouth opened. "Help me," she whispered with great effort, "Alex, help me . . ."

But Alex didn't know how.

Tears in her own eyes, she patted Kiki's bony arm and hurried out of the room.

Something was very, very wrong here. Not wrong like someone attacking Kyle and throwing him off the deck . . . *that* was a criminal act. This was . . . this was different. Beyond ordinary . . . beyond criminal . . . what was happening to Kiki had no logical, reasonable explanation. Even if she *were* anorexic, she wouldn't have lost that much weight that fast. Not possible.

Kiki had wished . . . had wished to lose weight. Julie had wished that her face wasn't so "ordinary." Gabe had wished he didn't have to walk so much. And Marty had wished he didn't have to give his speech. Kyle had wished for peace and quiet.

And all of their wishes had come true in a horrible, twisted way.

If only the doctor could find a logical, scientific explanation for Marty's loss of speech. Then she would know that what she was thinking was totally crazy, that her imagination was running away with her.

If not, she knew where she had to go.

The doctor found nothing wrong with

Marty's throat. "Stage fright's my guess," he said when they emerged from the cubicle. "Shouldn't last long."

But Alex knew it wasn't stage fright. And not just because Marty wasn't the type . . . there was more to it than that. Kiki wasn't the type to starve herself, either, but there she lay in that bed, a shrunken skeleton.

What was happening to them had nothing to do with logic or reason. Whatever it was, it was beyond their control. Maybe beyond *anyone's* control. Except . . .

Alex couldn't believe what she was thinking. Crazy, crazy. . . .

"I'm going to Vinnie's," she told Marty as they left the infirmary. "Want to come?"

He shook his head. He rummaged in his pockets for a piece of paper. Finding one, and a pencil, he scribbled, *Going to bed. But I'll drop you off there first.*

"Thanks," she said.

When they reached Vinnie's, Alex started to get out. Marty suddenly tugged on her arm and held out two things. One was a scrap of paper.

Alex took it and read it. It said, *Found this under the seat of my car. Thought you might like to have it.* And then he handed her the second thing.

It was a tiny gold football.

Alex stared at it. It was dull and scratched and dusty. It had definitely been rolling around under the seat of a car . . . *not* lying safely in a brown envelope.

Marty hadn't stolen Kyle's smooth, shiny football from the hospital. And he hadn't left his in the bottom of a plant on the sixth-floor observation deck.

The smile she gave him then was dazzling. He brightened, and, returning her smile, scribbled quickly, *You're welcome. I hope you take better care of it than I did.*

"I will," she promised, giving him a hug.

He was smiling as he drove off.

Alex turned toward the restaurant. She knew what she had to do.

Taking a deep breath and squaring her shoulders, she started walking. She entered the restaurant and headed straight to the back.

There was no one at the red booth when she reached it.

Alex looked The Wizard full in the face and whispered, "What are you doing to my friends?"

Chapter 18

The pale, bearded face stared back at Alex, its glassy blue eyes cold and unseeing.

"I *said*, what have you done to my friends?" she repeated.

Nothing.

If anyone came in and saw her talking to The Wizard, she'd be carted away to a padded cell.

But she wasn't giving up. Some of the things that had been happening could have been the work of a maniac. After all, she had seen with her own eyes someone throwing Kyle off that deck, and it certainly hadn't been The Wizard. There had been something odd about him, about his arm, but it wasn't that the arm was mechanical. That had been a real person, she was sure of that. The accident *could* have been just that . . . an accident following a bad storm. And the driver of the shuttle bus . . . well, she couldn't be sure *what* was under that raincoat.

It *could* have been the same nut case that tossed Kyle.

But there were too many other things that couldn't be explained. How could someone steal Marty's voice and most of Kiki's body weight?

If, crazy as it seemed, The Wizard *had* heard the things they'd said when he first arrived, and *had* granted their wishes, then . . . oh, God, she *was* losing her mind . . . then maybe he could hear *her*.

If he was willing to listen. . . .

"Answer me, damn you!" Alex hissed. "I want my friends to be all right! Why are you *doing* this?"

There was another moment or two of silence. And then the familiar whirring and clanking began and the arm lifted . . .

And as it did so, Alex saw again the scene on the observation deck of the tower, saw Kyle's attacker pointing at him, and saw what she hadn't been able to remember before: the arm he was pointing was much longer than his other arm.

She looked carefully at The Wizard. Both his arms were the same size.

Besides, she was sure that Kyle's attacker had been a real, flesh-and-blood person.

She didn't know anyone whose right arm was longer than the left.

A card appeared in the little cup on the outside of the booth.

Alex didn't want to reach for it. She was afraid. She was so afraid that her palms were icy with sweat and her fingers felt too stiff to move. But she needed answers . . .

Breathing erratically, she picked up the card. And read, YOU HAVE GONE TOO FAR.

This was no common, garden-variety fortune from a machine. He was talking to *her*.

So. She'd been right. He *could* communicate.

Knowing she'd been right strengthened her resolve. "No," she said, staring straight into the cruel face, "*you* have gone too far. You have to stop, right now. You have to give Marty back his voice and make Kiki well. Do you *hear* me?"

And, just for a second, she thought she saw his eyes move, just a little bit to the right. Then her knees turned to butter as the clanking and whirring began, faster this time. The arms lifted up and out and another card shot into the cup.

YOU DARE TO THREATEN ME? She'd barely finished reading it before another card shot into the slot, and then another, the arms moving furiously, accompanied by a rushed but agonized creaking.

NO ONE DEFIES ME.

YOU ARE FINISHED.

For just a second, Alex faltered. Look what he had done to Marty and Kiki, and here she was, daring him, on her own, with no backup.

And at that moment, as if she had wished aloud, someone said, "Hey, Alex, you playing with that thing again?"

The cards still in her hand, Alex whirled to see Gabe approaching. She was surprised to see him back on crutches. Smiling, he leaned against the wall, lifted the right crutch and pointed it at her, saying, "You're going to go broke on that thing."

And as he pointed the crutch at her, Alex knew why, in the dim light on the tower's observation deck, Kyle's attacker had seemed to have an unusually long right arm.

He had been pointing a crutch at Kyle.

Chapter 19

The Wizard had fallen silent.

"Gabe," Alex said hesitantly, "what . . . what are you doing here?"

"Bummed out about being back on these wooden walking sticks," he said, moving toward her. "Thought maybe this place would cheer me up. I'm told I should have my head examined for playing on Saturday. Coach blames himself, but I'm the one who told him I was fine."

He was still smiling. He looked so sweet, so friendly . . . and Julie loved him, and Julie wasn't stupid . . .

"It was you, wasn't it? You tried to kill Kyle . . ." Alex began.

Gabe raised the crutch, lifing it high in the air.

Alex took a step backward, heard a sound behind her, began to turn around . . .

And then something slammed against the side of her head and everything went dark.

Chapter 20

Alex awoke to utter darkness. And silence. Her head ached. She was half-sitting, half-lying on a cold, hard floor.

Where *was* she?

What . . . what had happened?

She lifted a hand to touch the place on her head that hurt. Her fingers came away wet and sticky. Blood.

And she remembered, then. Gabe . . . the crutch . . . something had hit her . . .

Using the wall as a support, she stood up, and reeled with dizziness. Still holding the wall, she made her way forward, hand-over-hand, searching for a door. There had to be a door.

Her hand closed around a doorknob. It turned easily.

Slowly, carefully, she turned the knob all the way. Slowly, carefully, she pushed the door open, a quarter of an inch at a time. Where was Gabe? Waiting, outside this place . . . a closet, wasn't it? . . . to attack her again? Or had he gone, made his escape before she could come to?

As the door opened wider, light came in. Enough light for her to see that she was in a small closet. The shelves were piled high with empty white pizza boxes and fat packages of white napkins wrapped in clear plastic. A fishing pole leaned against the wall in the front corner.

She was in Vinnie's storage closet.

But . . . there was no sound coming from outside the open door. Silence . . . only silence. The quiet of an empty restaurant.

Alex's heart sank. Everyone had gone home, even Vinnie? She was here alone?

Or *was* she?

The phone . . . the phone was on the wall outside the closet. If she could get to it, if he wasn't waiting just outside the door for her . . . she could call the police.

No . . . no . . . too risky . . . too scary . . . he might hit her again before she could even dial . . .

You have no *choice*, Alex, she told herself. You can't stay in this closet forever. The telephone is *right there*. Go for it!

Taking several deep breaths, Alex pushed

the door open all the way, but remained in the doorway, afraid to move. . . .

And found herself staring directly into the face of The Wizard.

A wave of dizziness assaulted her, and she swayed, putting one hand to her head.

When the dizzy spell had passed, she looked to each side of her. There was no one there. Gabe had gone. She was alone. She could call the police and they would take her out of here and go arrest Gabe. At last she would be safe.

Then a voice said, *"It is your own doing."*

Alex jumped and stumbled back against the closet door. The knob jabbed her in the small of her back, and she cried out.

"You brought all of it upon yourself by doubting me," the voice continued. It was deep and cold and . . . Alex shivered . . . inhuman. *"No one doubts the power and goes unpunished."*

There was *no one* in the alcove.

No one but her and . . .

She wouldn't look at him. She *wouldn't*!

"It was I who summoned up the terrible wind that tormented you high above the ground," the voice went on, *"and it was I who locked the door to your little booth, and I who banished all light and removed the means for you to seek aid."*

She wouldn't answer it. Since he wasn't really speaking . . . because how *could he be?* . . . she wouldn't answer. None of this was really happening. She wasn't really standing in this doorway. She was, obviously, still unconscious, lying on the floor of the closet.

Then she remembered Kiki, lying in the infirmary bed, wasting away, and Marty, stricken into silence. Gabe couldn't have done *that*. No human could.

Alex lifted her eyes. And met his.

They were no longer cold, icy, marble-like. They glowed, hot, hot, blazing blue, red around the edges, and they were fixed on her . . . angry, glowing eyes fixed on her. . . .

"I never did anything to you," she said defiantly, although her body trembled and her hands felt like ice.

The voice rose to a roar that shook the red metal booth. *"You doubted! You questioned my power! And then ridiculed your friends for their faith in my power."*

Alex shrank back against the door. "I . . . I didn't mean. . . ." Then Kiki's skeletal face appeared in her mind, and she stood up straighter, angry again. "Kiki didn't doubt you. And look what you did to her."

The voice quieted. *"I only gave her what she asked for."*

"You're *killing* her!"

"*Your friends are idiots. Never satisfied. Wishing for foolish things, failing to appreciate what they already have. It was time they learned a lesson.*"

"They've learned it! You have to stop it now! Give Marty back his voice, make Kiki well."

"*And if I choose not to?*"

"I'll . . . I'll smash you to bits, I will, I swear!" Alex's eyes scanned the small alcove for something . . . a tool of some kind. There had to be something. . . .

And that was when she saw the crutch. Just the tip of it. Poking out from behind The Wizard's booth.

Gabe. He hadn't left, after all.

Her first instinct was to run. For the front door. It would take him some time to make it out from behind that booth.

But if the door was locked, she wouldn't be able to get out. And then he'd be on her . . .

There had to be another way . . .

Without making a sound, Alex took several small steps backward and, with her right hand, reached behind her to grab Vinnie's fishing pole from its corner.

Curling her fingers carefully around the edge of the hook, Alex said softly, "You can come out now, Gabe. I know you're behind The Wizard."

The crutch moved slightly.

"You have to come out, Gabe. Because I'm going to the phone now and calling the police."

And she did exactly that. She turned, pulled a quarter from her jeans pocket, and deposited it, keeping her eyes on the crutch.

The coin had barely clinked into place when the crutch moved again, and this time, it was picked up off the ground and used as support for the figure that emerged from behind The Wizard.

Alex dropped the receiver and let it dangle, but not before she'd managed to punch the "O."

"Gabe," she began, and then stopped.

Because it wasn't Gabe who emerged from behind The Wizard.

It was Bennett.

Chapter 21

"Bennett?" Alex said, her fingers relaxing on the fishing rod. "Where's Gabe?"

Bennett, resting on his crutches, leaned against The Wizard. "Taking a nice, long nap, just like you." He shook his head. "Tried to interfere. Can't have that, can we? He didn't seem at all happy that I'd sent you sleepy-bye. Came right at me with that crutch of his. I barely had time to toss you in that closet. Bad timing on my part. If I'd known he was going to show, I'd have waited for a better time. Oh, well, these things happen."

"You . . . *you* hit me?"

"Of course. You thought it was Gabe? Gabe wouldn't hurt a fly, Alex. Everybody knows that." His eyes on her face, Bennett began humming, *The wheels on the bus go round and round, round and round . . .*

"That was you, too? You were driving the bus?"

"Yep. Quite a ride, wasn't it? Stole that bus right out of the campus parking lot. Driver left the keys in it, went off to get a cup of coffee. I should report him."

"Why weren't you hurt? When you jumped off? We were going so fast . . ."

He grinned. "Football padding, lots of it. And a helmet, under that rain hat."

Alex thought hard, her mind racing over everything that had happened. "Oh, Bennett, no . . . *you* threw Kyle off the tower?"

Bennett stiffened. "Had to. It's what The Wizard wanted. We thought, The Wizard and I, that I could just *will* Kyle off that tower. You know, borrow The Wizard's power. But it didn't work. So I had to throw him off." Bennett shuddered. "It was awful."

Yes, it was. Her hands tightened on the fishing rod. "And you're the one who stole Kyle's football charm from the envelope in the hospital?"

"Had to. I remembered that I'd given mine to that stupid girl." Bennett's upper lip curled in contempt. "She gave it back, and I lost it that night on the tower. I told you it was home, in Utah, but I knew if anyone asked that girl, she'd say I'd had it here, on campus. So I helped myself to Kyle's." Bennett laughed. "It's not as if he *knows* it's gone."

"And you gave Julie that mirror?"

Bennett looked blank. "Mirror?"

"What did you do to Kiki? How did you make Marty lose his voice?"

His face registered total bewilderment. "Alex, *I* didn't do any of that. I don't have that kind of power." He nodded toward The Wizard. "It was him. I did the rest of it, though. For *him.*"

"Him?"

"Well, you don't think I'd do something like that to Kyle on my own, do you?" He looked wounded. "Gee, Alex, I thought you *liked* me. Not as much as you like Marty, of course, but . . ."

"I do, I did, Bennett, but . . ."

"Well, I *had* to do it," he said. He nodded his head toward The Wizard, implacable beside him. "*He* said it was the only way I could play football again. He'd make my knees better if I did what he said." Bennett brightened. "And he *did*, Alex. You saw me in that game Saturday. My knees were fine."

"Then why are you on crutches now?" she said sharply.

He flushed. "Well, I have to keep doing stuff for him. Every time I did something he asked me to, my knees got better. But they didn't *stay* better." His expression became sullen. "It's not like I *want* to do all this stuff, Alex. I *have* to."

"No, you don't. We're all your friends, Bennett. Football's not more important than friends, is it?"

Then he shouted at her, "If I hadn't played football in high school, I wouldn't have *had* any friends! I was *somebody* in high school because of football. I was important. And when I couldn't play anymore, all of that stopped. I *hated* that! I couldn't believe it was all ending so soon. And," he glanced gratefully at The Wizard, "then I found out it didn't have to. I could play again. All I had to do was teach a few people a lesson or two. But then," he said, glaring at her, "you *saw* me . . . on the tower, with Kyle."

"And you had to kill me? Oh, Bennett. . . ."

"You would have *told*! Anyway, Alex, The Wizard's right, about the others, I mean. They're never satisfied. Always wishing, always wanting more . . . they *needed* to be taught a lesson."

It was too insane, too crazy. . . . Bennett had done it for *The Wizard?* Crazy . . .

But The Wizard had communicated with *her*, too, hadn't he?

"How . . . how did he tell you what he wanted you to do?" she asked.

"Alex," Bennett said impatiently, "don't you know anything about mental telepathy? The Wizard has lots of different powers. Mental telepathy is only one of them. I know what he wants. And he knows what I want."

Alex tried to think. She couldn't talk to Bennett rationally. He'd gone over the edge, and she pitied him. But he had hurt her. And she had a feeling he intended to do worse. He had such a strange expression on his face. She had to do *something*.

"How are your knees now, Bennett?"

He flushed again. "Pretty bad. That's why . . . well, I don't want to do this, Alex, you know I like you. You're okay. But," he shook his head, "The Wizard won't help me again unless I do him another favor. And you made him awfully mad. So," Bennett's eyes gleamed, "the favor that he wants this time is getting rid of you." He began moving toward her. "I don't have any choice, Alex." There was pain in his face, but she could tell that it had nothing to do with her. It was clearly physical pain. He was leaning on his crutches so heavily, she knew his knees were killing him.

But that wasn't stopping him. He continued to advance.

I'm sorry, Bennett, she thought as she lifted the fishing pole and slashed it sideways, knocking his crutches out from under him.

Crying out, he tumbled sideways, slamming with full force into the metal booth behind him. There was a dull thud as his head hit. The booth shook. Bennett moaned, his eyes closed, and he slid to the floor, unconscious.

Just as Alex moved to grab the phone and call for help, The Wizard's eyes caught hers. They were blazing again, a brilliant, heated blue that stopped her in her tracks. And a voice that wasn't Bennett's roared, *"You will pay! You will pay!"*

"No!" she screamed, as the booth began to rock wildly, whirring and clanking so loudly her eardrums felt like they would burst, "No, I won't!"

And grabbing up one of Bennett's crutches, she drove it through the glass of the booth. It shattered, glass flying everywhere, some of it landing in The Wizard's tall silvery hat. The arms began waving frantically. The eyes rolled wildly. Crying, her hair flying around her face, Alex thrust the heavy crutch through another pane of glass, then another, and another, and when those had shattered, she drove it through the one remaining pane of glass.

When the glass was gone, she used the

crutch on the pale-faced Wizard, hammering, pounding, slashing away. She hammered the nose away, watching the plaster crumble with satisfaction, slashed at the open red mouth until it disappeared, pounded at the cheeks, and then, in one final, desperate blow, smashed the head into a dozen pieces that fell, harmless, into the bottom of the booth.

The blazing blue eyes were gone.

The Wizard was no more.

Crying, drained, still holding the crutch, Alex sank to the floor.

Chapter 22

The stadium was packed. The marching band had spelled out SALEM U on the field. Half-time was nearly over.

Kiki leaned over and drew a handful of chips from the package in Alex's hands. "So, are we going to win this one or what? Think Marty'll play at all? I heard him begging the coach when I passed the bench on my way to get my hot dog."

Alex nodded, fingering the small golden football worn on a chain around her neck. "Of course we're going to win. And Kyle, Marty, and Gabe will probably all play. In the final minutes, like last week."

"So," Julie asked, "are we going to Vinnie's after the game to celebrate?"

Alex could hear Vinnie's mentioned now

without trembling. She had thought that would never be possible.

But she knew now that anything was possible.

Anything. . . .

Epilogue

"Hey, that's pretty neat," the man in the gray overcoat and dark hat tells the antique shop owner. "That wizard thing over there in the corner. What'll you take for it?"

"That'll come pretty dear," the owner replies. "Genuine antique, you know. Had to put all new glass in it, but otherwise it's in tiptop shape. Works, too. Full of them fortune-telling cards."

"Tell you what," the customer says, taking out a cigar and lighting it, "if we can strike a deal, I'll take it. Opening up a hamburger place out there near the State University. The kids'll get a big kick out of something like that." He laughs. "They're not afraid of the future the way we old folks are. Let's sit down and talk turkey."

They sit at a table. At no time do they look up and see the cold, blue eyes watching their every move, listening to their every word.

And so they do not see the red lips curve slightly upward.

Return to Nightmare Hall

. . . if you dare.

The Scream Team

"We're number one!"
"We're number one!"
"We're number one!"

In the darkened room, the participants in the regional summer cheerleading camp flickered across the television screen. Scream teams from colleges all over the state did splits, flips, pyramids, jumps. They clapped their hands and stomped their feet and chanted enthusiastically.

And through it all they kept smiling and making it look easy. That was the most important part of all. To keep smiling. To make it always look easy.

The remote control clicked.

Freeze frame.

Yes. There they were. The Salem junior varsity, distinctive in their red-and-white uniforms. They were all smiling. They were all making it look easy.

But I knew it wasn't.

I knew the horrible truth of what had happened to them.

I must have moved. With a faint rustling, the tattered pom-pom in my lap fell to the floor.

Bending and picking it up, I stroked the ragged strands gently, gently. In the flickering light from the screen, the dark stains on the red heart of the pom-pom had no color.

But by the light of day, I knew, they were the color of blood.

I clicked the remote again.

Forward.

Freeze frame.

I lifted the pom-pom. Breathed softly, softly on the blood-soaked heart of it as if inhaling the scent of some fatal flower.

I caressed the deliciously death-stained strands delicately.

Had the Salem junior varsity cheerleaders been smiling when they died?

Would the new scream team make death look easy?

I clicked the remote one last time.

The screen went dark.

Freeze frame . . .

forever.

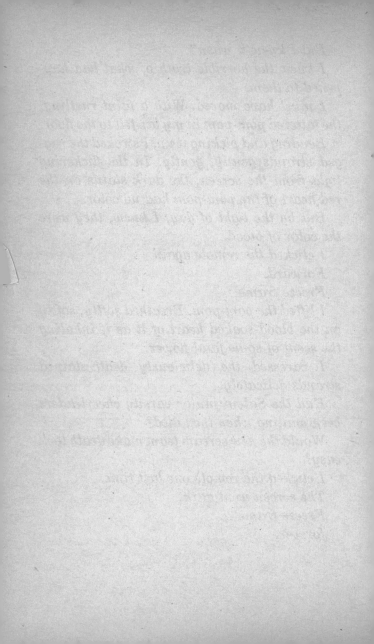

About the Author

"Writing tales of horror makes it hard to convince people that I'm a nice, gentle person," says **Diane Hoh**.

"So what's a nice woman like me doing scaring people?"

"Discovering the fearful side of life: what makes the heart pound, the adrenalin flow, the breath catch in the throat. And hoping always that the reader is having a frightfully good time, too."

Diane Hoh grew up in Warren, Pennsylvania. Since then, she has lived in New York, Colorado, and North Carolina, before settling in Austin, Texas. "Reading and writing take up most of my life," says Hoh, "along with family, music, and gardening." Her other horror novels include *Funhouse*, *The Accident*, *The Invitation*, *The Fever*, and *The Train*.

About the Author

THRILLERS